"This sort of looks like the land west of the Three Rivers Ranch house. Where you showed me the North Star. Remember?"

Remember? Those moments had been burned into her memory. Even if she never saw him again for the rest of her life, she'd always have those special moments to relive in her mind.

The thought unexpectedly caused her throat to tighten and she wished the waitress would get back with their drinks. She didn't want Jack to think she was getting emotional, especially because she could feel their time together winding to a close.

"I do. And I just happened to know a place not too far west of here where there's another special view of the evening star."

His eyelids lowered ever so slightly as he looked across the table at her. "After we eat, you should show me."

Did he expect her to look at him in the moonlight and not feel the urge to kiss him? Or maybe she'd get lucky, Vanessa thought, and the moon would be in a new phase and the light would be too puny to illuminate his face.

Damn it, Vanessa. Who are you fooling? You could find Jack's lips in the darkest of nights...

Dear Reader,

Stone Creek Ranch in southern Utah has always been home to Jack Hollister and his seven siblings. For more than fifty years, the family has successfully raised cattle and sheep, and as comanager with his father, Hadley, Jack has no desire to interrupt his work to travel down to Arizona to meet a family who just happens to have the same last name. But when Maureen Hollister, matriarch of Arizona ranching royalty, informs Hadley that her genealogy search has led her to believe the two families might be related, he immediately orders Jack to make the trip to Three Rivers Ranch.

When Jack arrives on the massive ranch, he isn't expecting to find relatives, much less a hot romance. He's already gone through one humiliating affair with a woman—he has no desire to try again. But these Arizona Hollisters are all about love and marriage. And beautiful schoolteacher Vanessa Richardson has more to her plan than drawing out the Hollister family tree. She has the idea that Jack needs a few lessons in love.

Before long, Jack is wondering if he truly has found another branch of the family. And where is he going to find the willpower to go home to Utah and leave sweet Vanessa behind?

I hope you enjoy meeting this new family of Hollisters and discovering how Jack and Vanessa learn how the word *home* simply means being together.

God Bless the trails you ride,

The Other Hollister Man

STELLA BAGWELL

HARLEQUIN
SPECIAL
EDITION

HARLEQUIN®
SPECIAL
EDITION™

Recycling programs
for this product may
not exist in your area.

ISBN-13: 978-1-335-72407-6

The Other Hollister Man

Copyright © 2022 by Stella Bagwell

For questions and comments about the quality of this book,
please contact us at CustomerService@Harlequin.com.

Harlequin Enterprises ULC
22 Adelaide St. West, 41st Floor
Toronto, Ontario M5H 4E3, Canada
www.Harlequin.com

Printed in U.S.A.

After writing more than one hundred books for Harlequin, **Stella Bagwell** still finds it exciting to create new stories and bring her characters to life. She loves all things Western and has been married to her own real cowboy for forty-four years. Living on the south Texas coast, she also enjoys being outdoors and helping her husband care for the horses, cats and dog that call their small ranch home. The couple has one son, who teaches high school mathematics and is also an athletic director. Stella loves hearing from readers. They can contact her at stellabagwell@gmail.com.

Books by Stella Bagwell

Harlequin Special Edition

Men of the West

The Rancher's Best Gift
Her Man Behind the Badge
His Forever Texas Rose
The Baby That Binds Them
Sleigh Ride with the Rancher
The Wrangler Rides Again

Montana Mavericks: The Real Cowboys of Bronco Heights

For His Daughter's Sake

Montana Mavericks: The Lonelyhearts Ranch

The Little Maverick Matchmaker

Visit the Author Profile page at Harlequin.com for more titles.

To my editor, Gail Chasan,
for allowing my Hollister family
to live on. I'm eternally grateful.

Prologue

Something out of the ordinary was happening on Stone Creek Ranch. Jack Hollister couldn't recall ever seeing more than three people at one time in his father's small study. This afternoon, however, ten adults were crammed into the room. Eight of them were Jack and his siblings, all of whom were standing around the front of a large oak desk. Seated in comfortable leather chairs behind the desk, their parents, Hadley and Claire, were exchanging dubious glances.

For the past minute, Jack and his four brothers, along with their three sisters, had been waiting patiently for their father to explain the reason for this sudden call for a family meeting. But so far the only words he'd spoken had been something in their mother's ear.

Now Jack sensed his siblings were starting to grow restless. Off to his left, he heard his twin sisters, Bonnie and Beatrice, let out matching sighs, while to his immediate right, Hunter, the eldest of the group, was shifting his weight from one cowboy boot to the other. Past him, Quint was making an issue of clearing his throat. As for Jack, he was normally a patient man, but this waiting around was stretching his nerves to the limit.

Pushing the brim of his cowboy hat back off his forehead, he looked over at Hunter. "I'm beginning to think Dad is losing it," he whispered to Hunter. "What the hell are we doing here? I have all kinds of work waiting to be finished by the end of the day. At this rate, it's going to be dark before we ever leave this room."

Hunter cocked a mocking brow at Jack. "Yeah, and I still have to haul fifteen bulls to Spanish Fork before I can think about quitting for the night. What is this about, anyway? If Dad thinks he needs to ask me about that land he has his eye on, then he's wasting his time. I don't give a damn."

"Really?" Jack retorted.

"Well, hell yes, really. In spite of you thinking Dad is getting dementia, he's kept Stone Creek Ranch working in the black for years now. I figure if he believes we should invest in more land, then we ought to."

Jack rolled his eyes. "Dad's mind is as sharp as a tack. I—"

Hunter's elbow suddenly gouged Jack's ribs as Hadley stirred and seemed about to speak. "Shh."

Jack looked away from his brother to the front of the room, where their father was tapping an ink pen on the top of the desk as though it were a judge's gavel. As he rose to his feet, the room grew so quiet Jack could hear the birds chattering outside the windows.

At age fifty-nine, Hadley Hollister was still an impressive figure of a man. Six foot three of hard, fit muscle and dark hair that had grayed slightly at the temples, his presence always filled the room. And Jack would feel certain in saying all of his eight children adored him. Even though there were times they didn't totally agree with him.

"First off, thank you all for making the effort to be here. I realize you all have responsibilities with your jobs, but after talking this matter over with your mother, we both agreed that everyone in the family needed to hear this at the same time."

"Dad, is this about buying more cattle and sheep?"

The question came from Cordell, the middle sibling, who was the foreman of the family-owned-and-operated ranch.

Grace, a medical doctor, who was a couple of years older than Cordell and standing on the opposite side of Hunter, groaned out loud. "Oh, for Pete's sake, Cord! Can't you think of anything else besides livestock—and women?"

The interruption caused Hadley to pick up a bronze paperweight in the shape of a horse and bang it forcefully on the desktop. Next to him Claire grimaced as she watched indentions appear in the varnished wood.

"That's enough! You siblings can't be together for five minutes before you're arguing like adolescents! I want everyone to remain quiet. When I'm finished you can throw all the questions you want at me." He reached down and picked up a long white envelope. "I received this letter a few days ago from Gil and Maureen Hollister. The couple have recently been digging into their family genealogy and believe our two families could somehow be related. They haven't found a concrete link between us—yet. That's why they're asking for our help. But Maureen, especially, seems to believe her husband is somehow related to me."

Jack did his best to stifle a mocking snort, but Cordell didn't bother to hide his opinion on the matter and burst out laughing.

"Cord, this might not be so funny," Hadley swiftly admonished. "Distant or not, relatives can create unwanted problems. Therefore, your mother and I have both decided this is a matter we can't ignore."

Nodding in agreement, Claire said, "Your father and I feel that if there's even the slightest chance that these Arizona Hollisters are relatives, then you all deserve to know it."

"And what if this is all a scam? What if these people are simply out for their own personal gain? You don't know any of them, do you?"

The questions had already whipped through Jack's thoughts. Thankfully, his younger brother Flint, who was a deputy sheriff for Beaver County, Utah, suggested the suspicion before Jack had to.

Hadley turned his attention to Flint, who was next to the youngest of his sons. "I've only heard of their ranch—Three Rivers Ranch in southern Arizona. I've spoken with Maureen on the phone, but I've never met anyone from the family or anyone who's ever worked for them. That's why I'm going to send one of you to Three Rivers Ranch to get a sense of what's really going on with this family. This woman has extended an invitation for a visit, and I've promised her that one of us would be there by the end of the week."

Jack and his siblings all exchanged shocked glances, but none of them expressed their feelings out loud.

Hadley continued. "I'm sure you're all wondering which one of you will be making the trip. So I'm going to go through the list by way of elimination."

Hunter was the first one to burst out a protest. "Dad, with the rodeo going on, the Flying H has to be in Spanish Fork for the next five days. There's no way in hell I can go!"

"Rest easy, Hunter. You were the first one I crossed off the list."

"I suppose just because Hunter owns the Flying H Rodeo Company means he gets an automatic pass." Beatrice tossed Hunter a cheeky look before she smiled sweetly at their father. "Well, that's okay with me. I'd love to go, Dad. I can certainly get away from my job."

Hadley gave the youngest of his children an indulgent smile. "I'm sure you could, Bea. But none of the cowboys on Three Rivers would be safe from you. So no. You've already been crossed off the list, also."

Beatrice's mouth fell open as she turned a reproachful look on her twin. "Have you been talking about me?"

Hadley quickly interrupted her. "No one has to point out the fact to me that men are your number-one priority, Bea. And before you complain any further, Bonnie is off the list, too. Dealing with a group of strangers would give her stomach ulcers. Plus, I need her here to keep the office running smoothly."

While Bonnie looked relieved, Flint spoke up. "Well, it can't be me, Dad. I can't get off duty. With Wade out with a broken ankle, we're already short-handed."

"I've already come to that conclusion, Flint," Hadley told him. "You're excused, and so is Quint."

"I am?" Quint practically yelled. "Why? Don't you think I'd like to get away from herding cattle or sheep for a few days?"

Being the youngest son, Quint was constantly griping about all the manual labor he put into the ranch and often expressed his desire to be something more than a rancher. Hadley had always made a point to never stand in his son's way, but so far Quint hadn't found the fortitude to leave the ranch.

"Quint, I'm sure you would like to get away from the ranch. You talk of doing just that often enough. That's the main reason you're not going. You don't necessarily represent what the rest of your family values most, and that's Stone Creek Ranch and the Hollister name."

Quint looked sullen, and Jack tried to scrape up some sympathy for his brother but couldn't manage to find any. Even though Quint was twenty-six, he still had some growing up to do before he could adequately speak for himself much less the family.

"So," Hadley continued, "that brings things down to Grace and Jack."

Unable to remain quiet, Jack said, "Dad, that's no choice. We all know that Grace is the diplomat of the family. She'd be the perfect person to meet with these *other* Hollisters."

"You're right. Grace is more than a diplomat. She's also a sharp judge of character. But she has patients who count on her to be in her office whenever they need a doctor. She also has a six-year-old son to care for. She has too many responsibilities to juggle already. So that leaves you, Jack. And frankly, I happen to think you're the best Hollister for the job."

Jack was so stunned it took him a moment to pry his tongue from the roof of his mouth. "Me? You have to be kidding, Dad. I'm not a people person. Especially people I don't know. Besides, I have so much on my plate already that I'll never catch up. Haying time is nearly here, and we've not yet got all the branding done. And what—"

Hadley held up a hand to interrupt Jack's argument. "I'm fully aware of your duties, Jack. And I'm fairly certain between myself and your brothers we can deal with the extra work."

"But Dad, I—"

"Look, Jack, your parents are asking you to do this for the whole family. All you have to do is meet these people and decide if they're sincere or trying to pull a con. Maybe get their hands on our mineral rights. Who knows what they might be thinking or planning?"

If his parents trusted him to handle this unusual task, then Jack couldn't let them down. No matter how much he disliked the idea of going to Arizona.

From the corners of his eyes, Jack could see both Beatrice and Quint eyeing him with resentment, while the remainder of his siblings appeared relieved that he'd been the chosen one.

"Okay, Dad. When am I supposed to go on this trip?"

Hadley answered, "As soon as you can pack your bags, son."

Chapter One

Jack had expected Three Rivers Ranch to be a large operation. Before he'd left home, he'd taken a thorough look at their website. The property was so massive that it extended from Yavapai County and into Maricopa. The cattle numbered in the thousands, while a top-notch horse-breeding program drew buyers from all over the west. Yet even being aware of the magnitude of the place hadn't quite prepared Jack for the sight that unfolded before him when he topped a short mesa and the ranch headquarters appeared on the valley floor below.

Braking his truck to a halt on the side of the dirt road, he took a moment to study the distant image of a huge, three-story house painted white and shaded by enormous cottonwood trees. Nearby a work yard consisted of several enormous barns, a multitude of loafing sheds, cattle pens and green paddocks dotted with countless horses.

Who were these people? And how the heck could they possibly be connected to his family? The questions rolled through his mind as he eased his foot off the brake and drove the last bit of dusty dirt road to Three Rivers Ranch.

A circle drive brought Jack to the front of the house, where he parked his truck near a white-board fence. Presently there were no other vehicles around, but he figured with a place this size, the family and workers parked elsewhere and left this shaded area in the front for visitors.

By the time he'd climbed out of the truck and fetched a single duffel bag from the back floorboard, he spotted a woman hurrying across the porch and down a set of wide steps.

With his bag in hand, he skirted the truck and walked over to meet her.

"Hello," she called to him. "Welcome to Three Rivers."

Tall with a strong, trim figure, she wore a battered brown cowboy hat that covered most of her chestnut hair, which was pulled into a low ponytail. She was dressed in ranch work clothes, and from the looks of the dust on her blue jeans and roughout boots, she must have recently been in a cattle pen.

Who was this lady? One of the Hollisters' ranch hands?

"Hello," he replied. "If this is Three Rivers Ranch, then I made the right turn about twenty miles back."

Her smile was beaming. "The county roads do make a maze of forks before you reach the ranch. I'm happy you chose the right one. The Utah plates on your truck tell me you have to be Jack."

"Yes. I'm Jack Hollister."

"It's so nice to meet you, Jack. I've been anxious for your arrival. Actually, we've all been looking forward to seeing you. By the way, I'm Maureen Hollister. I imagine your father has probably already told you about me."

"Dad only told me that you and your husband own Three Rivers and that the property has been in your family for a long time," Jack told her.

She continued to smile at him. "A Hollister first established the place in 1847. So yes, that's quite a long time."

He set his bag on the ground, then reached to shake her hand, but she had other ideas. She grabbed both his hands and squeezed them tightly.

"Forgive me, Jack, but a mere handshake won't do."

To say Jack was stunned would be putting it mildly. This was Maureen Hollister? The matriarch of the family? She hardly looked old enough to have six grown children. Attractive, strong and earthy, she was the epitome of a working cowgirl. That had him suddenly thinking of his own mother: Claire was the exact opposite of this woman. She'd always been more of a fragile flower, one that their father had pampered over the years. Even if she'd been willing to try, she'd never hold up to strenuous outside work. Much less endure this fierce Arizona heat.

Before he could think of a reply, she continued. "You're probably thinking I'm crazy, too, the way I keep staring at you, but your eyes—they look exactly like Chandler's eyes. He's my second-to-oldest son."

Jack hardly knew how to respond to that. Was she serious? He decided it might be best to treat her comment lightly. "Well, I imagine your son is a lot better-looking than me."

Laughing, she gave his hands one last squeeze before she dropped her hold on him and stepped back. "You don't need any improvement in the looks department. Chandler is a handsome devil, too. He also happens to closely resemble my late husband, Joel. But—" with a shake of her head, she released another soft laugh "—we'll talk about all of that later. Right now, you must be exhausted from the long drive. Let's go in. The men should be coming in from the ranch yard soon and you can meet all of them over drinks. I imagine you could use one of those right about now."

Just being here and meeting Maureen had left Jack a little loopy. No telling what a beverage or two might do to him, he thought ruefully.

"Sounds nice," he said. "The drive was a long one."

She slipped her arm through his, and after he'd picked up his bag, she led him in the direction of the house. "We've just finished a roundup last week, and we're still doing some branding. That's why I'm covered in dust. We've not had rain in weeks. But I expect you know what it's like to go through a drought."

"We mainly depend on snowfall to put moisture in the ground," he replied, while wondering if Maureen Hollister was this handsy with all her guests. She was treating him like a relative she'd not seen in years. And maybe he was, Jack thought, then immediately gave himself a hard mental shake. The notion that he and his family might be related to this set of Hollisters seemed too incredible to consider.

"Snow is a rarity around here. Every winter Gil and I take the grandkids up to Flagstaff to spend a day or two in the snow. Otherwise they wouldn't have a chance to make snowballs or go sledding." As they walked across the shaded yard, she glanced over at him. "Do your parents have grandchildren?"

"One. A six-year-old boy. He belongs to my sister Grace."

She tossed a sly smile at him. "Hmm. Eight children and only one grandchild. You must be a shy bunch."

He cleared his throat. "I think, uh, *cautious* would be a closer description."

She laughed. "You sound just like my sons, back before they all married and started having children of their own. They were cautious, too. Until they met the right woman."

Jack could've told her he wasn't expecting to meet the right woman. Nor was he looking for one. He'd gone down that path before, and he wasn't about to put himself in a position to be duped and humiliated again.

The two of them climbed the steps to a covered porch that ran the full width of the house. The plank floor was painted the same gray as the wide steps. Wicker lawn furniture with bright cushions was grouped at both ends of the porch, while several wooden rockers sat facing a northern view of the desert mountains.

"So your father tells me you co-manage Stone Creek Ranch with him," she said. "Is that something you want to do? Or was the job thrown at you because you're the best man available? That's how it was with my son Blake. After his father died, Blake had to take over the management end of things here on Three Rivers. He didn't necessarily want the position. But he does a heck of a job at it."

"I like what I do," he replied. "I guess you could say I enjoy being able to tell Dad what I think our ranch needs or doesn't need."

With a knowing little chuckle, she opened a wide wooden door and gestured for him to enter the house. "You just don't like it when your father sends you off on a wild-goose chase. Right?"

Jack wasn't one to blush, but he could feel heat

stinging his face and throat. This woman was reading him easier than a first-grade primer. Was he that transparent? Or was she merely that good at sizing up character?

"I try to do my family duty."

His remark appeared to surprise her, and then she smiled and clapped her hands together. "Oh my, this is just—incredible! You couldn't sound more like my Blake if you tried. And your eyes are the spitting image of Chandler's! I'll be honest, Jack. I never expected this."

Neither had Jack. Maureen Hollister was simply seeing things in him that she wanted to see. Or she was trying to make him believe they were truly related. But why would she want to do either of those things? What would be the gain? This Hollister family hardly needed more land or money. Or could be she was the type who enjoyed a big family and considered the more the merrier.

"I don't want to seem disingenuous or negative, but I—"

With a shake of her head, she said, "You don't have to explain, Jack. You have all kinds of doubts and questions swirling around in your head. And that's a good thing. So do I. So do the rest of my family. We'll have plenty of time to hash out all of that later. Right now, I want you to get comfortable. I have a room all ready for you upstairs. You can take your time freshening up before drinks and dinner."

"Thanks. That sounds good."

He followed Maureen into a short entryway before they entered a long sitting room furnished with plush leather furniture and several antique tables. The scent of lemon wax drifted to his nostrils, along with the sharp odor of fresh-cut marigolds. Except for the faint sound of music coming from somewhere else in the house, he heard nothing except the light tap of their boot heels against the cypress wood flooring.

As though she was reading his mind, Maureen said, "Our nanny, Tallulah, has all the kids upstairs in the playroom. That's why the house is so quiet here on the main floor."

Maureen and Gil's brood had so many children that a nanny was required to help take care of them? Jack couldn't imagine such a situation at Stone Creek. Not with him and his brothers vowing to remain single.

"How many grandchildren do you and Gil have?" he asked.

"Fifteen. With two more about to be born any day. Blake's wife, Katherine, is having another set of twins. They'll be the third twins in the family. Naturally we're all excited for them to arrive."

"Fifteen! Do they all live in this house?"

She laughed. "Don't worry. Only five live here on the ranch."

He followed her into a long hallway, which had tongue-and-groove walls that were painted a celery green and the same cypress flooring as the sitting room. Several feet ahead of them, he could see a wide mahogany staircase leading to the upper floors of the house. He was wondering if Maureen was going to be taking him up those stairs when a door just beyond the landing opened and a tall, young woman with long black hair stepped out of the room.

Without glancing in their direction, she headed down the hallway. Maureen didn't hesitate to call out to her.

"Van, wait a minute! I have someone I want you to meet."

Halting in her tracks, the woman turned and joined him and Maureen at the bottom of the staircase.

Jack told himself not to stare, but his gaze refused to look anywhere but straight at the beauty standing in front of him. Dressed in worn blue jeans and a white shirt with the sleeves rolled back on her forearms, she was tall, long-legged and curvy. Her eyes were a luminous blue and framed with thick, sooty lashes. A straight little nose led down to a luscious set of berry-colored lips, while her shiny hair waved in a ponytail down her back.

"I'm glad we ran into you, Van," Maureen said. "I was just about to show our guest to his room upstairs. And since you two will be spending some time together, I thought you might want do the honor."

He'd be spending time with this woman? The

question was making a wild dash through Jack's head when he felt Maureen's hand on the back of his arm, nudging him forward.

"Jack, this is Vanessa Richardson," she said. "She's a schoolteacher and a longtime friend of the family. I hired her a few weeks ago to work on the Hollister family tree. So for convenience, she's been staying here on the ranch with us. While you're here, you two should find plenty to talk about."

The black-haired beauty extended her hand to him, and as Jack wrapped his hand around her soft fingers, he wondered if the long drive from Utah to Arizona had numbed his brain. What else could be making him feel addled?

"It's a pleasure to meet you, Ms. Richardson."

Maureen turned to Vanessa. "Van, this is Jack Hollister, the man from Stone Creek Ranch."

"I'm happy to meet you, Mr. Hollister," she told him, then cast a bewildered smile at Maureen. "Sounds strange, doesn't it? Another Mr. Hollister."

"It's going to take some getting used to," Maureen agreed. "But I'm sure Mr. Hollister won't mind a bit if you call him Jack. I've already taken the liberty."

He said, "I won't mind at all. And with several Mr. Hollisters already here on the ranch, it'll save some confusion."

"Thanks," she said. "And call me Van, if you'd like. All my friends do."

Realizing he was still hanging on to her hand,

Jack forced himself to release his hold on her fingers and take a step back.

"Well, now that you two have met, I have a few things I need to attend to before dinner. So I'm going to let Van show you upstairs," Maureen said, then turned her attention to Vanessa. "His room will be the one next to yours. Jazelle has it ready, but if there's anything else he needs, you can let her know."

Maureen quickly strode away, and Vanessa gestured toward the staircase. "This way, Jack. Your room is on the second floor."

"Next to yours," he couldn't help but add.

Her faint smile was a bit impish, and Jack decided he was going to like this woman. Probably more than he should.

"Don't worry," she said. "I promise to be a quiet neighbor while you're here."

He could've told her she'd already disturbed him, but he kept the thought to himself. For one thing, Jack wasn't a flirt. At least, he'd never thought of himself as one. Moreover, he wasn't in the market for romance. Not even a very brief one with a sexy young schoolteacher with a playful smile.

He said, "I doubt you could be rowdy enough to disturb me."

She slanted him an amused look. "Did you have a nice drive down?"

"It was uneventful. That was the best thing about it."

"Hmm. Sounds like you don't like traveling. Or you weren't all that keen about making this trip."

"Honestly, I'd rather be home, doing what I do best," he said bluntly.

"And what is that, exactly?"

"I co-manage our family ranch with my father."

She darted a meaningful look at him. "Strange, don't you think? Maureen finds a Hollister family that might or might not be related, and you turn out to be ranchers just like them."

It was strange, all right, Jack thought. So were the odd feelings this woman was causing him. "I wouldn't call us *just like them*. We're not in the same league as these Hollisters. From what I've seen so far, this is…quite a place."

"These Hollisters are hardly up against it," Vanessa said as they reached the landing on the second floor. "I'm anxious to hear what Stone Creek Ranch is like, but for the moment I'm not going to pester you with questions. No doubt your head is buzzing right now."

Yeah, it was buzzing with thoughts and questions about her, he thought wryly.

Clearing his throat, he said, "Trust me. Our ranch in Utah is nothing like this."

She gestured toward a hallway to their right. "I've been to Kanab and part of Monument Valley. Is that area anywhere near your ranch?"

"About two and a half hours north of there and west of Beaver."

He followed her to the end of the hallway, where

she opened a door and motioned for him to follow her into the room.

"I've never been in this room before," she admitted as her gaze encompassed the spacious bedroom. "This is nice."

The furniture was rough-hewn pine worn smooth from years of use. Judging by the soft patina of the wood, Jack figured the heavy pieces had been made long before Jack had been born. The bed was queen-size and covered with a chocolate-brown comforter. Accent pillows of beige and rust were piled high against the headboard. Drapes of the same shade of brown framed a double window located several feet beyond the foot of the bed.

As Jack walked over to peer at the view, Vanessa moved alongside him. Her nearness allowed him to pick up the faint scent of her perfume. The smell was soft, mysterious and alluring and reminded him of a desert mountain trail at twilight.

"Looks like Maureen thoughtfully chose this room for you," she said. "She knew you'd appreciate a bird's-eye view of the ranch yard."

Grateful that her voice interrupted his wandering thoughts, he studied the scene beyond the pane. Directly below was a section of green lawn with what looked to be a children's play area equipped with an elaborate jungle-gym set and an equally large sandpile. A hundred or so yards beyond the yard fence, he could see cowboys on horseback moving cattle from one holding pen to another. Yellow Cur dogs circled and nipped at the heels of the cows and calves, while dust boiled high over the work area.

"Does that scene make you feel a little more at home?" she asked.

"It's a pretty sight. But I won't feel at home until I get back to Stone Creek Ranch," he said, then feeling remorseful, added, "Sorry. That didn't exactly sound…gracious, did it?"

"It sounded truthful. Nothing wrong with that."

She turned away from the window and walked over to a door on the opposite side of the room. After pulling it partially open, she peered around the edge. "Looks like this is your private bath. I see plenty of towels, and I'm sure you'll find all kinds of soaps and toiletries. But if there's anything else you need, let Jazelle know, and she'll get it for you."

"And Jazelle is?"

She shut the bathroom door and rejoined him at the window. "Jazelle is the housekeeper. You'll meet her when you go down for drinks. She's married to Connor Murphy, a deputy sheriff for Yavapai County. He's a partner to Deputy Joseph Hollister, who's Maureen's youngest son."

Jack felt the hair on the back of his neck stand up. "There's another odd coincidence. I have a younger brother who's also a deputy sheriff."

Her brows lifted. "Wow. I'm beginning to hear spooky music."

"Strange coincidences do happen."

"Sure, they do." A clever smile on her lips, she headed toward the door. "See you later, Jack."

Once the door closed behind her, Jack felt as if the air had suddenly swooshed out of him.

His father hadn't mentioned that a woman had been hired to dig into the family genealogy. Could be Hadley hadn't known about Vanessa Richardson, Jack thought. Or maybe he had known and had decided not to share the fact with Jack.

But even if Hadley had mentioned Vanessa, there was no way Jack would've been prepared for the woman. Besides being beautiful and sexy, she was also intuitive and just a bit flirty. Or had he just imagined that last part?

Hell, it didn't matter, Jack thought. He wasn't here to spark up a romance. He was here to meet these Hollisters and try to determine if there was any kind of connection between the two families.

And as far as he was concerned, there wasn't going to be any kind of connection developing between him and the pretty schoolteacher. Even if, by some wild chance, she wanted it to.

Chapter Two

Jack was finishing a second margarita before he felt the tequila begin to convince his nerves to calm and the taut muscles in his neck and shoulders to relax.

It wasn't like him to be edgy. Even when he was out of his element, such as he was this evening with the Three Rivers Hollister family gathered around him. But when Jack had joined them in the den for cocktails, he'd expected a flurry of questions about past and present relatives to be thrown at him.

And he wasn't quite ready to admit that his father's family had been splintered for years. Especially when this group of Hollisters appeared to be so close-knit. Yet so far, the only questions they'd tossed at Jack were about Stone Creek and the methods he and his family used to work the ranch.

"Would you like another bourbon and cola, Holt?"

The question came from Jazelle, the young blonde housekeeper Jack had met some forty-five minutes ago when he'd first entered the den. Presently she was standing in front of Holt's chair to Jack's left.

Chuckling, Holt cocked a playful brow at the woman. "Are you trying to get me in trouble, Jazelle? Isabelle is sitting on the opposite side of the room, but she has an eagle eye. One bourbon only. I'm not about to break the promise I made to my wife. Especially after the hell she went through while she was pregnant with little Wes."

Jazelle gave the horse trainer an approving wink. "I was only testing you a little, Holt." She looked at Jack. "In Holt's younger days, this guy used to down several bourbons before dinner. Now that he has three sons, he's a lot smarter."

"And a lot happier," Holt confessed.

"No need to remind us, Holt. That possum grin on your face makes it clear that you're happy," she teased.

Jack studied the horse trainer. Unlike his three brothers, Holt's hair was a rusty-brown, and his eyes were green. All the Hollister men, including Gil, were tall and lean and physically fit. But Holt had that extra hardness that came from long hours spent in the saddle.

"You have three sons?" Jack asked him.

Holt's grin grew deeper. "Carter, Axel and Wes. The oldest is two and a half, the middle one is fifteen months, and the newest addition is nine weeks."

"And Isabelle, the mother, is also a horse trainer and rancher. Holt should have told you that, too."

The remark came from Chandler, the veterinarian of the bunch. He was sitting next to Holt in a deep leather armchair. From the moment Jack had met him, he'd found himself studying the man's eyes and trying to see the resemblance Maureen had mentioned. So far the only comparison Jack found was the same vivid blue color.

"She must be a strong woman," Jack said, while thinking he couldn't imagine his mother being so mentally or physically capable. But then, Hadley had spent years spoiling his wife, Jack thought.

Chandler lifted a daiquiri from the tray Jazelle was carrying before he looked over at Jack and grinned. "She has to be as strong as nails to live with my little brother."

Holt let out a mocking laugh. "Oh, and I guess you're going to tell Jack how easy you make life for Roslyn? She works hard as your assistant at the animal clinic all day, then comes home and corrals your two kids. And let's not forget that Billy is more like having three boys than one."

"That's right. He behaves just like his Uncle Holt," Chandler retorted.

Shaking her head at the two men, Jazelle stepped

over to where Jack was seated in a padded armchair. "Would you care for another margarita, Jack?"

"No, thanks. I wouldn't want everyone to see me stagger into the dining room."

Her smile was a bit empathetic, and Jack figured she understood how out of place he felt among all these strangers who just happened to have the same last name as his.

"Well, just let me know if you'd like anything else," she told him.

The housekeeper moved on to Blake, who was sitting in an armchair on Jack's right. With his boots propped on a footstool and his eyes half-closed, the ranch manager appeared content to let everyone else do the talking.

"What about you, Blake? Another margarita? You've had a busy day. Might do you good."

Blake chuckled. "Thanks, Jazelle, but I'm afraid I'd be like Jack suggested. Staggering into dinner or half-asleep."

"Well, I popped into the kitchen about five minutes ago, and Sophia says dinner is almost ready."

"Great. I hope she and Reeva made plenty. I haven't eaten since five this morning. And have you seen Kat? When we came downstairs she went to the kitchen, and I haven't seen her since. What is she doing? Eating before she eats again?"

Jazelle laughed. "Blake, don't you dare scold Kat for eating. She's feeding two extra little mouths, you know. Anyway, she's not in the kitchen. She and Van went out to the patio. A couple of the ranch hands were going to build a fire in the firepit, and the two women wanted to oversee the job, I think."

So that's where Vanessa had gotten off to, Jack thought. Ever since he'd entered the den, he'd been wondering where she was and watching for her to make an appearance. He was beginning to think she'd probably left the ranch for the evening. Most likely on a date with one of the single cowboys. The fact that his assumption had been wrong lifted his spirits considerably.

Jazelle moved over to where Gil and Maureen were sharing a love seat. Next to them, Joseph, the deputy sheriff and youngest of the brothers, had pulled up a chair.

So far Joseph hadn't spoken all that much to Jack, and a few times he'd felt the younger Hollister eyeing him furtively. No doubt the lawman in him was suspicious about Jack and his motives for being here. If the situation was reversed, Jack's brother Flint would be reacting in the same guarded manner.

"We're about to start haying in the lower meadows," Gil said to Jack. "The land has to be irrigated. Otherwise, we'd be looking at scrub vegetation and no grass. Do you irrigate on Stone Creek?"

"On some areas of the ranch we irrigate. We're fortunate enough to have the Beaver River running through a section of our property. Plus, we get quite a bit of snow during the winter months. Thankfully, it gives us deep moisture. However, we only grow a portion of the hay we use. We don't have the man-power that you do here on Three Rivers, so we buy part of our hay from a dealer in Nevada."

Holt chuckled. "We have several hay meadows, plenty of irrigation and manpower to get it all done, but Blake still ends up buying alfalfa."

"And who causes that?" Blake fired back at Holt. "Those damned horses of yours are nothing but hay-burners."

Maureen frowned at her eldest son. "Blake! You're going to make Jack think you brothers argue all the time."

"I expect Jack has already figured out that we joke around with each other," Blake told his mother. "I imagine that he and his brothers probably do the same thing."

"Actually, Jack, we argue like hell over some things," Holt said. "But we usually end up coming to an agreement."

Blake chuckled. "Especially when I tell Holt to go ahead and buy all the horses he wants. That's how to make my little brother happy."

"We only keep a remuda of about fifty horses," Jack informed them. "Each year we usually pick out ten of the best mares and breed those. That's the ex-tent of the ranch's horse allowance."

"Count yourself lucky, Jack," Blake joked. "If I could control Holt's horse addiction, the ranch would have enough money to start up three banks."

Holt groaned loudly, while the remaining family

members laughed. Jack was wondering if this bunch was always in such a lighthearted humor when he noticed a pair of French doors on the opposite side of the den swing open.

Vanessa and Blake's very pregnant wife, Katherine, stepped into the room, and as the two women walked toward the seated group, Jack tried not to stare at the sexy schoolteacher. But when her smile fastened directly on him, there was no way he could ignore her or the way his heart jumped into a quick, heavy thud.

"It's cooling down nicely outside, and the guys have built a lovely fire for us," Katherine announced as she slowly eased a hip onto the arm of her husband's chair. "Maureen, what do you think about having dessert on the patio tonight? The kids are all begging to roast marshmallows and make s'mores. I thought it might make up for them not eating at the big table tonight."

"Sounds good to me," Maureen said. "That is, if our guest can put up with a few rowdy kids."

From the corner of his eye, he noticed Vanessa had skirted around the back of their chairs and was now standing just beyond Blake and Katherine. Would she be sitting with her friend at the dinner table? he wondered. Or would he be lucky enough to maneuver her into sitting next to him?

"Don't worry about me," Jack told Maureen. "And I hope you're not keeping the kids away from the dining table just because I'm here."

Blake and Chandler both let out loud groans.

"Jack, you have no idea what you're saying," Chandler said. "Presently, we have five children in the house. I say presently because Blake and Kat will soon make it seven. Ten more children belong to our siblings who live off the ranch. Even with only the five around the table, we couldn't hear ourselves speak. Trust me. Before you head back home to Utah, you'll see what I mean."

Strange, Jack thought. As he was driving down here to Three Rivers, he'd already been thinking wistfully of the day he'd be headed back north to Stone Creek. But looking at Vanessa and the way she was smiling at him made leaving just a dim spot at the back of his mind.

"Dinner is ready, everyone," Jazelle announced from the open doorway of the den.

"Finally," Holt said. "My stomach is about to cave in."

Jack swallowed the last of his drink and was searching for a place to set his empty glass when Holt solved the problem by plucking it out of his hand and placing it next to the tumbler he'd left on an end table.

"Don't worry," he told Jack. "Jazelle will gather up everything. She keeps us all spoiled."

Jack wouldn't know about being spoiled by a housekeeper. They'd never had one at Stone Creek. His mother hired a lady that came in twice a week to do the deep cleaning. Otherwise, there was no one to serve them drinks and dinner. Everyone helped themselves from pots on the stove, and he and his siblings took turns helping their mother clean up the kitchen.

"She seems very efficient," Jack said for lack of anything better.

Holt grinned as though Jack had just told a joke. "Efficient? She's more like a lifesaver."

The group began to file out of the den, and Jack found himself walking alongside Gil and wondering if it would look too conspicuous if he paused long enough to catch Vanessa as she walked by.

"I hope you like Mexican food, Jack," Gil said to him. "Reeva's gotten into an early Christmas spirit and made a pile of tamales. I think you'll find the food delicious."

"I love Mexican food," he told him. "And I am hungry."

An arm suddenly linked to his, and Jack looked around to see Vanessa had slipped up beside him. Surprise and joy splintered through him as he spotted her tempting smile.

"I'm the only woman here without an escort," she said. "Do you mind being mine?"

"My pleasure, Vanessa."

Her arm tightened ever so slightly on his, and the contact shot a shaft of heat from his elbow all the way up to his shoulder.

"Did you know that tamales are a celebration

dish?" she asked. "That's why Gil associated them with Christmas, even though we're only in August."

Jack's attention was so wrapped up in her lips he very nearly missed what she was saying. "A celebration? No. I didn't know. Why are tamales considered festive?"

"The corn. A necessary and much-loved staple by the Mayans and Aztecs. History hasn't changed much over hundreds of years. In the southwest we still love our tamales on special occasions—like a visitor from Utah," she added with a coy smile.

She smelled just as she had earlier this evening when she'd showed him to his room, but she didn't look quite the same, Jack noted. Now she was wearing a black sleeveless dress that buttoned down the front. The waist was belted with a gold chain, and the hem reached to a few inches above her knees. The ponytail she'd been wearing earlier this afternoon had been let down, allowing her black hair to swing freely against her back. She was far too sexy for his peace of mind. Yet she hardly seemed aware of the potent effect she was having on him.

"You obviously like teaching," he said as he tried to ignore the flush of heat that had somehow found its way to his face. "What other kind of lessons can I look forward to while I'm here?"

She laughed softly. "I only teach history."

"I never was very good at that subject."

"What was your best subject? Recess?" she teased.

"How could you tell?"

She laughed again, and the sound caused something to do a little flip in the pit of Jack's stomach.

"I seriously doubt that you were an indifferent student. In fact, I'm guessing you were a studious kind of guy. Otherwise, you wouldn't be helping your father manage your family ranch."

The pleasure he felt from her compliment was downright silly, and suddenly without warning, Jack was thinking back to those days he'd behaved like a besotted fool over Desiree. After that painful fiasco, he'd vowed to never let himself be so stupid over a woman again. But there was no need to be rehashing that hard-learned lesson now. In a few days he'd be back in Utah. Which meant there wouldn't be enough time for him to make a jackass of himself over Vanessa.

"I have a degree in ranch management," he told her. "I didn't necessarily want to go to college for four years. But I did it to please my parents. And because I wanted to be better educated for my job. Now I'm glad I endured all those classes."

Smiling, she gave his arm another little squeeze. "I'm glad you did, too."

By now they'd reached the open doorway to a spacious dining room. The oak table in the middle of the floor was long enough to seat twenty people; however, tonight there were only twelve place settings. Five on one side, six on the other and one at the west end.

"Jack, you're going to sit between Van and Chandler," Maureen said as the family began to take their respective chairs. "And don't be bashful about yelling out if you want anything."

"Thank you, Maureen. I'm sure I'll have more than enough."

Vanessa's hand released its lock on his arm, but the loss of her touch was only momentary as her hand promptly wrapped around his.

With a slight tug on his fingers, she urged him to the right side of the table. "We sit over here, Jack. And lucky us. We get to face the windows and look out."

Since the sun had already fallen, he wasn't sure what they could possibly see beyond the panes of glass. But the view hardly mattered. With Vanessa at his side, it was going to be difficult to keep his attention on anything except her.

Once everyone was seated, the dishes of food rapidly made their way around the table, and as Gil had promised, everything tasted delicious.

"The Hollisters have two cooks," Vanessa said as she forked up a bite of cabeza and flour tortilla. "Reeva and her granddaughter, Sophia. The food they prepare is so good I can hardly resist stuffing myself. I told Maureen I was going to have to start jogging a few miles to keep the pounds off, and she suggested I follow her around for most of the day. Ha! If I tried that I'd lose more than a few pounds. More like the use of my arms or legs."

"Sounds serious," Jack replied. "Maureen must live a dangerous life."

She chuckled under her breath. "Not to her. But it would be extremely dangerous for me. She spends the majority of her days atop a horse. And I'm not that adept at riding."

"Why not? All you need is good balance and core strength."

She flashed him a smile. "What I'm lacking is nerve."

Jack couldn't imagine this woman lacking confidence. "Handling a horse is nothing compared to a roomful of students. You need to get over your fears."

She looked over at him, and Jack found himself studying the smoothness of her tanned complexion, the faint sprinkle of freckles across the bridge of her nose and the clear blue color of her eyes. Even with a minimal amount of makeup, she looked beautiful and vibrant.

"You're probably right," she said. "I should get over my fear. Of horses and—a few other things."

He wanted to ask her about those *other things* but decided the question was too personal. Jack wasn't like his brother Cordell. If he was here in Jack's place, he would've probably already asked Vanessa for a date. Thank goodness their father had been smart enough to keep the Romeo of the family back on Stone Creek, he thought.

For the next few minutes everyone appeared to concentrate on eating, and the conversation on Jack's end of the table lagged. Until Chandler said in a voice only meant for Jack's ears, "In case you've been wondering why Mom is sitting at the end of the table and Gil is sitting kitty-corner from her instead of at the other end—it's because of Dad."

Glancing over at the veterinarian, Jack said, "Actually, I was curious as to why the chair at the end of the table is empty. But I figured Gil wanted to sit close to Maureen. They do appear to be extra close."

Chandler's smile was wry. "Make that heavy on the extra. Don't get me wrong. I mean that in a good way. We're all very glad about Mom and Gil. He's made her happy again, and that's all that matters."

"And the empty chair?" Jack asked.

"Was where our father, Joel, always sat. No one has sat there since he died. Or I should say, since he was murdered."

Murdered? His father hadn't mentioned anything sinister happening to this family! "Oh, I'm sorry. I—didn't know."

Chandler shook his head. "Dad was killed because he tried to help a woman get out of a bad situation. He was the sort who'd lend a hand to anyone who asked. And what made the whole matter worse, it took us a long time to learn what actually happened to him. At first his case was ruled an accident, then years later, after we discovered evidence, it was re-opened and labeled a homicide."

When Jack had first arrived on Three Rivers, he'd thought this family's problems, if any, amounted to no more than getting their cattle to market or dealing with a searing drought. He'd never imagined them going through such a tragedy. Which only proved that being rich didn't shield a person from sorrows.

Not wanting to sound trite, Jack kept his reply simple. "Must've been tough on all of you."

"Yeah. Especially Mom. But all is better now."

Jack glanced down the table toward Maureen and Gil. The Hollister matriarch had changed into an ankle-length skirt and silky blouse for dinner and tied her chestnut hair back with a matching scarf. She hardly looked like the same woman who'd greeted Jack this afternoon on the front lawn.

"Your mother has the idea that you and I resemble one another," Jack told him, then realized a little late that his comment would probably open a can of worms. But hell, he couldn't put off the inevitable or ignore the elephant in the room any longer. After all, learning if the two families were related was the reason for him being at Three Rivers. It certainly wasn't to make eyes at a sexy teacher, he thought, as he tried his best to keep his gaze from slipping over to her.

Chandler grinned as he dipped a chip into the pile of guacamole on his plate. "And I look a lot like my dad. But Mom sees things in people that it takes me much longer to recognize." He turned his head and made a pointed survey of Jack's face. "Frankly, I'm thinking we do favor one another just a bit."

Nerves pricked the back of Jack's neck. Hearing Maureen make the suggestion was one thing, but coming from Chandler himself was altogether rattling.

"Does that worry you?" Jack asked cautiously.

Chandler laughed and slapped a reassuring hand on Jack's shoulder. "If that's all I had to worry about, I wouldn't have any concerns at all."

Chandler's reaction wasn't at all what Jack had expected, and suddenly he felt a sense of relief wash over him. It was becoming clear to him that Chandler and his siblings didn't want anything from him or his family. Neither did Maureen and Gil. They were only curious as to whether the two branches of Hollisters had originated from the same tree. Just as his own parents were curious.

Vanessa leaned her head out over her plate and looked in the two men's direction. "Hey, you two. If you're telling jokes, I want to hear," she said. "I can use a laugh, too, you know."

"No jokes," Chandler told her. "Just a man thing."

"Well, man thing or not," Roslyn spoke up from the other side of Chandler, "if it's funny we all need to hear it. Especially after the afternoon we had at the clinic."

From her place at the end of the table, Maureen looked at her daughter-in-law. "What happened at the clinic? Anything we need to hear about?"

Chandler's wife suddenly grew tearful and quickly dabbed a napkin to her eyes. "Honey, you tell her," Roslyn said to him. "I don't want to start bawling."

He gave his wife an indulgent smile before explaining to everyone around the table. "A stray dog—a pregnant dog at that—was hit by a vehicle. Thankfully a Good Samaritan picked her up and brought her to the clinic. She and the babies are going to be fine, but Roslyn had a tough time helping me deal with her injuries."

Katherine immediately jumped up from her chair and hurried around the table to wrap a comforting arm around Roslyn's shoulders. "Oh, Roz, you poor thing. Don't cry. Chandler's the best. He'll make sure she and the babies are okay."

Roslyn gave Katherine's hand a grateful pat and reassured her sister-in-law that she wasn't going to fall to pieces.

While Jack observed the interchange between the two women, he wondered what the ranch house at Stone Creek would be like if he and his brothers had wives and babies. Moreover, how would it be to have a woman in his bed? A woman like Vanessa?

Jack's thoughts must have wandered longer than he'd thought, because he suddenly realized that Katherine had returned to her chair, and Maureen was looking down the table and straight at him.

"Now that Chandler's story has made us all want to start bawling, would you like more food, Jack?" she asked. "Or maybe another margarita?"

The questions made everyone laugh, including Jack.

"No, thanks, Maureen. It's all very delicious, and

I've had more than enough tequila," he said. "However, there is something I'd like to say to everyone."

"By all means, Jack. Please feel free to say whatever you'd like. We're a thick-skinned bunch around here. Roslyn just proved that," she added jokingly.

After another round of chuckles, Jack said, "Well, I want to thank you all for making me feel so welcome. To be honest, before I got here, I wasn't sure what to expect."

"Aw, come on and admit it," Holt spoke up with a teasing grin. "You didn't want to come down here in the first place."

Jack felt a wash of hot color streak up his neck and onto his face, while next to him he could feel Vanessa watching him intently.

"Not at first. But now that I've met all of you, I'm glad Dad sent me on this trip."

"We're all glad you're here, Jack," Gil told him.

Jack's gaze encompassed the whole group seated at the table. "You've all been gracious about not badgering me with questions about my family. But you don't have to be so nice. I don't mind talking about my relatives. At least, the ones I know well enough to talk about," he added. "Some of them—a couple of uncles and a few cousins on my father's side I've only seen a few times in my life."

"Same here, Jack," Joseph spoke up. "We have some relatives we've only heard about but never met."

"Actually, there is something similar about your family and mine," Jack remarked. "You have twins."

Katherine laughed as she rested a protective hand on the top of her very rounded tummy. "Vivian and Sawyer have a set of boys. Blake and I already have a set of a boy and girl. Now we're expecting another set."

Jack nodded. "I have identical twin sisters. They're twenty-four, the babies of the family. And I have twin cousins. Although, I've not seen them in several years."

Katherine turned an incredulous look on her husband. "Blake, did you hear that? Twins in the family! What could it mean?"

Chandler answered for his brother. "As a doctor, I believe it means we've all drunk water west of the Continental Divide."

The veterinarian's remark produced chuckles around the table, and then Blake said, "I'd say the twin thing is an odd coincidence. But there will be plenty of time later for Jack and Vanessa to go over the family-tree business. As far as I'm concerned, I'm more interested in hearing how he manages Stone Creek."

"And I want to hear about the sheep they raise," Joseph spoke up. "I wish Tessa could've come with me tonight. She would've loved to ask Jack all about Stone Creek's sheep. She's been considering buying a small herd to put on the land we purchased over by Camp Verde Reservation."

"Sheep! Are you serious?" Maureen asked her youngest son.

The question turned the dinner conversation from family relations to that of ranching, and for the next several minutes Jack very nearly forgot why he'd made this pilgrimage to Three Rivers Ranch.

Vanessa wasn't exactly happy with herself. Getting close to the Hollisters' guest from Utah wasn't a smart thing to do. It was true that she'd be the one going over the family tree with Jack, so she could hardly avoid spending time with the man. But that didn't mean she was supposed to stick to his side like their hips were attached with Velcro.

But from the very first moment she'd spotted Jack standing near the bottom of the stairs, something had gone a little haywire in her brain. Before he'd arrived, Maureen had told her he was thirty-six and single. What she hadn't warned her about was the rancher's striking good looks. Like a wild, majestic mustang, he was rough, strong and beautiful all at the same time. And as she'd shown him upstairs to his room, her senses had been overwhelmed by his masculine presence. She'd felt her cheeks burning and her heart pounding. Curiosity about him had overwhelmed her, and even though hours had passed since Maureen had first introduced them, she was still preoccupied with questions about him.

Why was a man who looked like him still single? Had he had a wife in the past and something had happened to end the marriage? Did he have children somewhere? Or a special girlfriend waiting for him

to return home? And why the heck did she want to
know all these things about the cowboy, anyway?

*Those questions about Jack shouldn't concern
you, Vanessa. The guy will be here for a week at
the most, and then he'll be gone. His life is in Utah.
Yours is here in Arizona. To have a hot little tryst
with him would be pointless and, even more, reckless. He's the kind that causes a bucketload of tears.
And you've already shed plenty of those over a man.*

"I don't know about you, but I'm totally stuffed."

Jack's voice interrupted Vanessa's wandering
thoughts, and she glanced over to where he was sitting next to her on a rock bench near the firepit. For
the past half hour, the adults had consumed rum-
soaked bread pudding, while the kids enjoyed making s'mores. And in spite of telling herself that she
needed to get up and mill about the small group on
the patio, she'd not left Jack's side.

"Maybe you need to go for a walk," she suggested.
"If you'd like, I'll show you one of my favorite night
views on the ranch."

As soon as the invitation had died on her lips, she
promptly wanted to kick herself. What had come
over her? She might as well get the word *brazen* tat-
tooed across her forehead.

"I'd like that." He stood and placed his empty dessert dish on a nearby table. "Do we need a light?"

Surprised that he was going to take up her offer,
she stood and tightened the shawl she'd thrown
around her shoulders.

"I've never needed one. My dad says I'm nocturnal and can see like a cat."

"I imagine you've saved plenty of money by not having to buy flashlights," he said.

She laughed. "Well, if it's pitch-black I might need a candle, but we still have a bit of twilight. And don't worry. If you start stumbling around in the dark, I'll lead you."

"Maybe you ought to lead me now," he suggested. "I have no idea which direction we're going."

Was he flirting? Vanessa didn't think so. He was just being companionable, she thought, as she looped her arm through his. An arm that felt as strong as steel and as hot as the forge it had taken to shape it.

"We'll go out this back gate," she told him.

Since they were already standing on the far back side of the patio, they didn't pass anyone as they stepped off the rock ground and into the shadowy yard. But she imagined that even if no one had seen them leave the patio, they would soon notice the two of them were missing.

Jack must have been thinking along those same lines as he said, "Do you think we should've told someone we were leaving?"

"No. They'll know we won't have gone far," she told him.

They stepped through a wooden gate, and then Vanessa guided him in a westerly direction away from the house.

"Do you stay here on the ranch very often?" he asked as they strolled over the moonlit ground.

"Only on special occasions. I'm only staying here now because of the genealogy work. I live in Wickenburg in a house I bought a few years ago. From here to there it's about a thirty-minute drive, and Maureen didn't want me to have to do that twice a day, so she insisted I stay here until I finish my research."

"And when do you plan to finish?"

"When I reach some sort of conclusion as to why the computer throws up Hadley Hollister's name when I'm working on Joel's past family."

"What if you can't find a conclusion?"

He couldn't know how much she enjoyed holding on to his arm and being close enough to pick up the spicy scent drifting from his shirt. Nor could he guess that he was the first man in a long time who'd piqued her interest.

She said, "I'm not one to give up. Unless I see that something is hopeless, then I'll concede. But I don't see this search as hopeless. At least, not yet."

"I'm having trouble seeing this search as anything more than a wild-goose chase. Even if you do find that our families are related, what is that really going to accomplish?"

She shrugged. "That all depends on the connection, don't you think?"

"You mean everyone ought to know whether a family member had a child out of wedlock and kept it a secret?" he asked. "I'm not so sure that dirty secrets should be revealed. Do you?"

His voice had turned a bit sardonic, and the change in him surprised her.

"What makes you think the connection might be shameful?" she asked.

He halted, and she turned slightly to look at him.

"Okay," he said. "Maybe I should have said it might be better to let sleeping dogs lie."

"Hmm. That's quite a change from your earlier attitude at dinner. You implied to the Hollisters that you were willing to go along with this family research. Have you suddenly changed your mind?"

"No. I guess I'm just thinking out loud and wondering if there's really a need for all this. We are who we are. Nothing is going to change that."

She smiled gently at him. "Right. So you have nothing to worry about, do you?"

He looked at her for a long moment and then laughed softly. "No. No worries. And I haven't changed my mind. I honestly do like these folks… and you."

Her heart was suddenly thumping hard and fast beneath her breast. "Thank you, Jack. I like you, too."

His face was lit with soft moonlight, and as she watched his gaze latch on to hers, she was overcome with the reckless urge to move closer, to slide her arms around him until she could feel his hard, warm body pressed against hers.

"I'm glad," he murmured.

Her gaze fell to the hard line of his lips. She hadn't kissed a man in ages. Nor had any desire to. Until now.

"Are you really?" she asked softly.

One corner of his lips twisted upward, and then his hands were on her shoulders. "Maybe I should show you how glad."

Instinctively, her palms came up and splayed against his chest. At the same time, heat from his fingers were burning through her shawl and spreading over her shoulders. "Jack, I...didn't bring you out here for this."

She watched in fascination as the half grin on his lips caused a dimple to carve a groove in his cheek.

"And I didn't come with you for this. But it's a good idea, don't you think?"

His voice had lowered to a rough whisper, and with each word he spoke, his face inched closer to hers. Totally mesmerized, her gaze focused on his lips.

"Um, maybe we should think first?"

"Why don't we just act first and think later? Hmm?"

"Good idea. Because right now—" closing her eyes, she angled her lips up to his "—my brain isn't working."

She felt his breath fan her cheeks, and then his lips were moving softly over hers. The contact was like a warm flame licking her face, inviting her to draw closer. Simultaneously, her mouth parted, and her arms slipped around his neck.

The taste and smell of him quickly invaded her senses, and as his hands slipped to her back and drew her tight against the front of his body, she realized that in all of her twenty-eight years, she'd never been kissed. Not like this.

And she didn't want the incredible connection to end. That wild thought barely had time to race through her mind before his mouth eased away from hers and he lifted his head to look down at her.

"My brain is working enough to tell me that was very nice, Vanessa."

Her lungs were starving for oxygen, but she didn't want to suck in a huge breath and have him thinking his kiss had literally knocked the air out of her. Even though it had.

"Van," she said thickly. "You agreed to call me Van, remember?"

"So I did. But I think Vanessa suits you better."

"Oh."

A vague smile curved the corner of his lips, and Vanessa was shocked by just how much she wanted to kiss him again. What was she doing? The man was a stranger! But oh, the touch of his hands, the warmth of his body and the taste of his lips felt as though she'd known him and wanted him all of her life.

"Now you're probably wondering why I kissed you," he murmured.

"Actually, I was wondering why I kissed you back," she said honestly.

Her reply appeared to amuse him, and Vanessa was relieved at his reaction. It wouldn't do for her to start thinking his kiss was meant to be serious.

"Why don't we just consider the whole thing as a getting-to-know-you kiss," he suggested.

"Is that what it was?"

"No. But I thought that would sound nicer than admitting I was just being a man who wanted to kiss a pretty woman."

And she'd reacted like a woman being kissed by a very virile man, she thought. Releasing another long, pent-up breath, she said, "Well, at least you're being honest about it."

The smile on his face turned a bit sheepish. "So do you still want to show me the view?" he asked gently. "Or would you rather return to the patio?"

She didn't have to think hard on his questions. Being alone with this man was making her feel incredibly alive and happy. And foolish or not, she wasn't quite ready for these special moments with him to end.

Chapter Three

"Sure, I still want to show you the view," Vanessa answered Jack in the most casual voice she could muster. "And give you a chance to walk off your dinner."

"Yeah. Like a pile of tamales worth of walking."

She reached for his hand, and they began to stroll forward. Ahead of them, the ground was mostly level with only a few Joshua trees and clumps of sage to maneuver around, but after a short distance an outcropping of huge boulders created a rocky hill.

"I'm guessing we're going to climb now," he said as they neared the base of the boulders.

"Only about halfway up. Otherwise, you won't get the full effect," she told him. "Are you game for climbing?"

He chuckled, and she thought how his laid-back attitude was so refreshing compared to Steven's sour mood swings. During the few months he'd been her husband, he had swung from hot to cold. When he'd asked her for a divorce before ever reaching their one-year anniversary, she shouldn't have been surprised. But in truth, she'd been stunned.

"Why not? I've let you lead me this far," he said. "I might as well go the whole distance."

She glanced at him. "Are you being agreeable just to be nice again?"

His brows lifted slightly. "No. I'm not always agreeable. And I figure I should be nice—to repay you for that kiss."

Thank goodness twilight was falling, she thought. Otherwise, he would see a hot blush creeping over her face. "I don't expect pay for the kiss. It was given freely, without charge."

He smiled. "Well, since you really want to know, I'm climbing the rocks with you because I want to."

Why in the world did his admission make her feel so good? It was downright silly. And it was especially foolish to let one little kiss go to her head. The brief embrace had meant nothing to Jack. It would be stupid to allow it to mean anything to her.

"Come on," she said.

With her hand still holding his, she urged him up a tiny trail she'd discovered one evening when she'd been exploring the area. It made the climb easy, and after a few short minutes, they reached another large boulder that created a natural bench.

"Now, how did this happen," Jack said, as he eyed the rock seating. "Did you bring a hammer and chisel up here and beat out this bench?"

She chuckled. "Do I look like a cavewoman, who needed to hack out a couch?"

His gaze swept up and down the length of her. "Well, you might if you were dressed in a fur bikini and sandals."

"That's an image born out of movies." She sat down on the bench and patted the space next to her. "This is where you'll see my favorite view. At this time of the evening, that is."

He eased down next to her, and Vanessa tried her best not to think about how close he was or how it had felt to be kissed by him.

"I probably shouldn't ask this, but why would you be out here at night—alone?" he asked, then as a thought seemingly struck him, he arched a brow at her. "Uh—or maybe you weren't alone."

Was he thinking she treated all men the way she'd been treating him? Inviting them on moonlit walks? Kissing them beneath the stars? She didn't do those things with other men, of course. But to admit that would be the same as revealing she considered him special.

Deciding she had to be truthful, she said, "Yes, I come out here alone. I like to have some quiet time by myself. And before you ask, I'm not afraid of stepping on a sidewinder in the dark. Snakes usually try to avoid humans. Besides, some humans are worse than snakes."

"That's true enough." He looked around him as though he was going to see an unusual rock formation or a thick stand of giant saguaros. "So what am I supposed to be gazing at now?"

She took his chin between her thumb and forefinger and turned his face straight ahead, then tilted it upward.

"Now look," she instructed as she forced her fingers to fall away from him. "See? A spectacular panorama of the North Star."

"Ah, it is pretty," he said, as he gazed up at the celestial display. "Lots of wide, inky sky and a big sparkling star. It's very beautiful."

Pleased that he seemed to appreciate the beauty, she said, "Since I've been staying here on the ranch, I've been enjoying stargazing. I can see them so much better out here than my place in town. The artificial lights kind of ruin the effect."

He studied the sky for a few more moments before his gaze turned back to her. "You seem to like living here on the ranch. That surprises me. I would expect a young woman like you to be bored living so far away from town, in the quiet countryside."

She laughed. "Quiet and boring? Three Rivers Ranch? Not hardly. This place is like a little town unto itself. From early morning until late at night, it's bustling. Is Stone Creek Ranch anything like this one?"

"Not really." He bent forward and plucked off a long piece of sage growing between the boulders below their feet. As he absently rolled the stalk between his palms, he said, "The only similarities are the wide skies and open range. But even those look a bit different. Here you have the big cactus and lots of chaparral. We have high desert mountains with grassy slopes and valleys. The big difference between this ranch and ours is that we only have a fraction of the land and cattle that Three Rivers owns. And the house is not nearly as big or grand. But as far as ranches go, Stone Creek is pretty and, more importantly, profitable."

His rugged profile was etched against the moonlight, and though she told herself to look elsewhere, she couldn't tear her gaze away from his face. "The pride I hear in your voice tells me it's a nice place. Do you like working with your family?"

He dropped the piece of sage, but she could smell the pungent odor from his crushing the leaves between his fingers. The scent matched him, she thought. Earthy, strong and enduring.

He said, "We're like most families, I suppose. We have our annoyed moments, but most of the time we enjoy being together. Quint, my youngest brother, does plenty of griping, but deep down he loves Stone Creek. He just doesn't admit it very often. Flint is a deputy, so he doesn't do a whole lot of ranch work. I guess you could say he's a lot like Joseph. He splits his time being a deputy and a rancher. My oldest brother, Hunter, owns and operates a rodeo company, the Flying H. So he stays on the road for a big portion of the year."

"That's interesting. How did he get into the rodeo business?"

"When he was young he rode saddle broncs. And he always enjoyed the rodeo life. You know, nomadic, pitting his skill against a twelve-hundred-pound animal. Hunter always was the type who liked a challenge. Dad never wanted Hunter to sink his money into a rodeo company. It's risky. But so far, he's made a success of it."

"You didn't want any part of helping him run it?"

He grunted with amusement. "No. I'm a man who likes to stay in one place. And my heart has always been in Stone Creek."

She studied him thoughtfully. "I imagine your father is glad about that."

"Out of the eight of us, I'm probably closest to Dad. Because our likes and wants are the same, I suppose."

"What about other siblings? Do they work on the ranch?" she asked curiously.

"Bonnie, one of the twins, does all the administrative work for the ranch. Beatrice has her own job in Cedar City. She's not the ranching sort. Grace, my older sister, is a doctor. She's a general practitioner and has her own practice in Beaver. And then there's Cordell. He's a middle child and the ranch foreman. We have five full-time ranch hands and hire extra day hands when we have big jobs like spring roundup."

"And your mother? Does she work?"

He said, "Not outside of the ranch. She used to say as soon as she got the twins into high school, she was going to get a job away from the ranch. But by the time the twins reached their teenage years, she decided a job outside the home wasn't that important to her anymore. Sometimes she helps Bonnie with the office work. And she dotes on Dad, so spoiling him keeps her busy."

"Hmm. Eight children," she said quietly. "Your parents must have a great marriage."

"I'd say most of their marriage has been good. They've had a rough patch or two. But that was only because the ranch was struggling and Dad was under a lot of stress." He slanted a curious look in her direction. "What about your parents? Do they live close by?"

"Phoenix. Which is close enough. I drive down and see them fairly often. Dad works for a financial investing firm, and Mom is a teacher."

He smiled. "And you followed her example."

"You could say that. I always liked being in the classroom, learning and helping others to learn."

Nodding, he said, "An admirable profession. Do you have siblings?"

"An older brother, Marcus. He has a wife and two

kids and lives over in California not far from his in-laws. He's a computer programmer."

"So you and your family all work with your brains. You must be an intelligent bunch."

"Well, you could say that about my parents and brother," she said wryly. "In the smarts department, I'm just average."

His gaze roamed her face, and she could only think how he might as well be touching her with his fingers. The idea left her cheeks burning.

"You're being humble now," he said.

She fought the urge to clear her throat. "No," she said. "I'm just being myself."

He looked away from her, and long seconds ticked by before he spoke again. Vanessa could only wonder what he was thinking. About getting back to Stone Creek?

"I suppose tomorrow we'll have to start going over the family tree," he said, his gaze fixed on the span of desert range in front of them.

"You don't sound very enthusiastic," she remarked. "Are you dreading it?"

He shrugged. "Before I arrived this afternoon, I thought I was going to dread the whole thing. But now, I'm thinking what the heck. This Hollister family doesn't seem like the judgmental sort. Neither do you."

"They aren't. And I'm certainly not. Why would you even be worrying over that sort of thing?"

"I'm not, actually. I mean, my family is what it

is. I can hardly change the situation. Some of my re-lations have split and splintered. Some I know very little about. I guess I came here thinking how nice it would be to say the Hollisters—that is, my Hol-listers—have always been a close-knit bunch. That all of them were people I could be proud to call re-lations. But that isn't the case."

"I don't need to hear about scandalous secrets or anything like that. Not unless you think it would help connect the dots of the family tree. Mainly I need names from you, and that will give me a big jump start. But like Blake said, we're not going to worry about that tonight. You just got here, and we—I—want you to enjoy it."

His gaze turned back to her. "That's nice of you, Vanessa."

Her heart was thumping too hard and fast for her peace of mind, and she knew if she didn't move away from his side, she was going to do something she would regret. Like reach for his hand and lift it to her lips. Or ask him to kiss her again.

Quickly, before she could let herself do either, she rose to her feet and drew in several deep breaths of cool night air. "Well, I, uh, guess we'd better start back," she suggested. "The others are going to think we've gotten lost—or something."

"Right. We should be getting back."

Rising to his feet, he gestured to the narrow trail they'd climbed. "You go first. I'll follow you."

Once they descended the rocky hill and started

walking in the direction of the house, Vanessa felt his hand casually settle against the small of her back. The sensation reminded her of so many things, most of which she'd tried to forget. Like how it felt to have a man at her side, touching her, helping her over the rough patches of life.

But that kind of togetherness didn't last. At least, not for her. And she needed to remember that no matter how good these minutes with Jack felt right now, they would soon be over, too.

Leaning against a painted-board fence, Jack gazed appreciatively at the blue-roan stallion ripping off bites of grass growing in a large paddock a hundred yards behind the horse barn. The animal was heavily muscled, while his shiny coat depicted his tip-top condition. Off to the left in a separate paddock, weanling colts and fillies were frolicking around the large grassy area like kids let loose on a playground.

The horse flesh on Three Rivers Ranch was extremely high quality. And as Jack watched the young horses, he thought about Blake and how he'd talked about keeping Holt happy by giving him a loose rein to buy the animals he wanted. The remark had made Jack think more than twice about his own position at Stone Creek. When it came to ranch expenses, he never considered whether his choices or decisions would ultimately make his brothers happy. Maybe that was part of the reason he and Cordell were often at odds and why Quint was outright resentful.

He was still mulling over the thought when his cell rang, and seeing the caller was his father, he quickly answered.

"Hi, Dad. How's your morning going?"

"Good. Only we've all been anxious to hear from you."

Jack let out a long breath. "Sorry, Dad. I should've already called. There's just so much to see and take in here."

Hadley said, "So is Three Rivers anything like you see on the website? And what about the Hollisters?"

Jack repositioned the cell phone against his ear as he peered once again at the roan stallion. "Dad, the website can't begin to give you the scope of this place. For instance, I'm standing here looking at a horse that would easily be worth six figures. But selling the animal will never happen. It's Holt's own personal horse—a pet. See what I mean?"

Hadley was silent for a moment, then said, "We'd already come to the conclusion that they were wealthy, Jack. Tell me something I don't know. Mainly, do you consider them a trustworthy bunch? If I thought for a minute they might be trying to lay claim to our land or the mineral rights, I would— well, I'd fight till my dying day."

Jack had spent a big portion of the morning riding horseback with Maureen and Gil and mixing and mingling with the numerous ranch hands who worked around the barns in the yard. So far everyone had treated him with warmth and respect.

"These Hollisters are all very down-to-earth. And they work as hard or harder than the hands they employ. As for being trustworthy, yeah, I'd trust them. And I really doubt they're cooking up a scheme to get our land or mineral rights."

"Well, coming from you, that's quite a statement."

Frowning, Jack asked, "What does that mean?"

"It's no secret that you have a cynical opinion of human nature. You don't easily trust people."

Jack couldn't deny his father's observations. He was cynical and mistrustful. He wasn't proud of the fact, but once he'd learned how Desiree had duped him into believing her lies, and then seeing her betrayal with his own eyes, something inside him had petrified to stone.

"It pays to be cautious, Dad. But this time… I don't have doubts. If you ever meet these folks, you'll see for yourself that they're genuine."

Hadley released a heavy breath. "I'm glad to hear it. So I'll put that worry to bed. Now, have you met with the woman who's working on the family tree?"

Met with her? Jack struggled to keep from groaning in his father's ear. What would Hadley think if he knew his son had already made a move on the woman? That he was acting like his brother Cordell?

"We, uh, met last night. She teaches high-school

history, so I feel sure she'll be good at digging into the past."

"And so far, what has she found concerning the two Hollister families? Anything more than what Maureen has already found?"

"We've not discussed anything about the family tree yet."

A long pregnant pause ensued before Hadley said, "I realize I told you to consider your time in Arizona a vacation, but what are you waiting on? Aren't you eager to get things started? To find some answers?"

Jack wasn't all that eager about any of it. He couldn't see the point. But he didn't want to disappoint his father.

"Sure, Dad. We'd all like answers. But the Hollisters wanted me to meet everyone and get settled before we got into the family-tree business. And frankly, I appreciate their thoughtfulness about the situation." He pushed back his shirt cuff and glanced at his watch. "Anyway, I'm meeting Vanessa in about thirty minutes, and she's going to show me what information she's dug up so far."

"Vanessa? Are you talking about the teacher?"

"Yes."

"I'm assuming she's not a member of the Hollister family. So what do you think of her? Is she trustworthy?" Hadley asked.

Jack slipped off his aviator sunglasses and rubbed his gritty eyes. He'd not slept well last night, and the restless hours he'd spent lying awake had little to do with being in a strange bed. At one point in the wee hours of the morning, he'd climbed out of bed and stood staring out the window at the ranch yard and had been surprised when he'd spotted a pair of ranch hands checking the cattle pens. Yet the momentary distraction hadn't been enough to make him forget the way Vanessa's face had looked bathed in moonlight. He'd been a damned fool for agreeing to take that walk with her. And an even bigger one for kissing her.

"She's a nice young woman," Jack answered, then asked, "And trustworthy? In what way do you mean?"

Hadley muttered a curse word. "Sorry, Jack. I don't know what's wrong with me. I sound like a suspicious old man."

Frowning, Jack said, "Listen, Dad. You sent me down here because you trusted me to deal with this family thing. Why are you suddenly so doubtful?"

"I'm not having doubts, son. I guess…not having you here makes everything feel different. I'm not used to you being gone."

"Cordell is there. So is Quint."

There was a long pause before Hadley finally said, "Cordell doesn't think like you. And Quint is, well, just Quint."

Grinning now, Jack slipped the sunglasses back onto his face. "Why, Dad, if I didn't know better, I'd say you were missing me."

"Hell, I am missing you!" Hadley's voice barked

in Jack's ear. "I made a mistake in sending you down there. I should've sent Cord or Bea."

Oh Lord, he didn't want to imagine what would've happened if it had been Cordell who'd strolled in the moonlight with Vanessa instead of Jack. And Beatrice would have taken one look at some of these ranch hands on Three Rivers and thought she'd walked into a candy store.

"No, you made the right choice. So relax. I'll be home in a few days."

"How few?"

Jack turned away from the paddock fence and started walking in the direction of the house. "We agreed on a week, at least, didn't we?"

"Yes. But if you see that the genealogy search is going nowhere before that time, then I want you to come home."

Jack wanted to gently remind his father that he was thirty-six years old and didn't need to be ordered about like a child. But he could tell, just by his words and the tone of his voice, that Hadley was a little lost without him on Stone Creek. The idea left Jack feeling loved and exasperated at the same time.

By the time he reached the house Jack's shirt was damp with sweat. August in the high desert valleys in Utah could be hot. But this heat was brutal, he thought. Although it was only midmorning, the sun was blazing like a blowtorch.

Deciding he needed to change into a clean shirt before he went to meet Vanessa, he hurriedly bounded up the stairs to his room. Yet as soon as he reached the landing, he saw Vanessa stepping through the door to her bedroom. She spotted him immediately and walked over to intercept him.

"Good morning, Jack. I was just headed down to Maureen's office. Were you coming up to get me?"

Shaking his head, he gestured to the damp spots on the front of his shirt. "I've been down at the horse paddocks and got sweaty walking back. I thought I'd better change."

She waved a dismissive hand at his shirt. "Nonsense. It's hot outside. If the men changed every time they got sweaty, that's all they'd be doing. You'll dry in a few minutes."

Surprised by her attitude, he said, "I don't want to stink up the room. Especially with you in it."

Chuckling, she looped her arm through his. "You won't. Come on. Let's go down. I think Jazelle is going to bring us some coffee. Have you eaten breakfast?"

"About four hours ago. I got up early and was surprised to find Blake and Gil and Maureen in the dining room and that Chandler had already left to go to his clinic."

Nodding, she said, "The family gets an early start to the day. Now me, I sleep a little later and take my breakfast in the kitchen. And sometimes I help Tallulah feed the kiddos."

"Sounds like you've been around here long enough to get familiar with the children," he said.

"I've been here close to a month now. Long enough to see Tallulah needs help at times."

He glanced at her. "Tallulah is the nanny. Am I remembering right?"

"Right. She's married to Jim Garroway."

"I met him this morning. He's a nice guy."

"I think so. He's certainly made Tallulah very happy."

As they descended the stairs together, Jack thought how during all those sleepless hours last night, he'd planned to keep a safe physical distance from Vanessa for the remainder of his stay here on the ranch. But those plans had gone to the wayside as soon as she stepped close to his side and looped her arm around his.

How in the world was he going to remain indifferent to this beautiful woman? He wasn't made of iron, he thought with chagrin.

Just think about Desiree, Jack. Remember how she smiled and kissed you and snuggled and promised she'd always love you? How much she talked about wanting to be your wife? And remember how she looked when you caught her making love to your brother Hunter? That should give you the strength to resist Vanessa or any woman.

Clearing his throat, Jack tried to ignore the taunting voice in his head. "Seems like most of the men here on the ranch all have happy women at their sides. What is it about this place? The food? The heat?"

She laughed softly. "Good question. Although, it hasn't always been full of happy hearts. But after Joseph and Tessa got married, it was like a domino effect. You'll see when I show you the family tree."

It wasn't like there'd never been a marriage among his siblings, Jack thought. Hunter had been married once for a couple of years, but his wife hadn't been able to deal with his nomadic life, and they'd parted. Thankfully, on amicable terms. Grace had been in medical school when she'd married Bradley. Two years later, she'd given birth to Ross, and Jack had believed his sister's marriage was stable, but he'd been wrong. Less than a year after Ross was born, Grace had filed for divorce.

No. There had been no happy hearts or domino effect for his family, Jack thought. And after his own humiliating failure at a serious romance, he had no intentions of trying the real thing. Which was a good reason for him to keep his distance from Vanessa, he thought. But was his willpower strong enough?

"Are you still with me, Jack?"

Vanessa's question managed to puncture his deep thoughts, and he glanced over at her. "With you?" he asked blankly.

"You looked like you were on another planet," she explained. "You must have gotten too much sun this morning."

He forced a chuckle. "Not really. I was just think-ing about my family back in Utah. We haven't had the domino effect you were talking about. Not yet, that is."

She cast him a wry look. "I don't expect that's an issue that keeps you awake at night."

It wouldn't do for this woman to know he'd spent most of last night with his eyes wide and his mind refusing to shut down, Jack thought. The reason for his sleepless hours hadn't been caused by thoughts of matrimony.

He said, "I have plenty of things to worry about other than me or my siblings getting married."

A knowing smile touched her lips. "I'm sure you do."

They reached the ground floor, and she guided him beneath the stairwell and down a short hallway. When they reached a wide door to their left, she pushed it open and motioned for him to follow her into the room.

"Maureen and Gil both use this study as an office," she explained.

"I spent part of the morning riding with them," Jack told her. "They were checking cattle on a range south of the ranch and thought I'd enjoy seeing the area."

"Did you?"

The landscape had been wild and rugged, and he'd enjoyed the ride. But seeing Vanessa again gave him far greater pleasure, he thought with a smile.

"Very much," he answered.

"I think I can safely say that Gil and Maureen

would both rather be outside doing ranch work than spending time in this office."

"When do they work in here?"

"Usually late at night before bedtime."

Jack glanced around the spacious room, which was equipped with two large oak desks paired with heavy leather executive chairs. Two of the four walls were lined with built-in bookshelves, while a third had windows that displayed a view of the northern mountain range. At one end, two stuffed armchairs, covered in hunter-green leather were separated by a small wooden table and lamp.

Like the rest of the house, it had an old-feel character. The cypress floor smelled of wax, and the moldings along the top of the ceiling and around the windows had been painstakingly carved by hand many years ago. Everything in the office, and the whole house for that matter, spoke of richness. Which made the whole idea of his family being related to these Hollisters seem even more far-fetched to Jack. Still, the realistic part of him understood that financial status had nothing to do with being blood related.

"I have some things on computer and some are on paper. Over here," she said, as she motioned to the desk closest to the window. "You might want to pull a chair up next to mine so you can see the monitor."

Glancing around, he spotted a pair of straight-backed wooden chairs sitting in one corner of the room. While he carried one of them over to the desk, she sat in the executive chair and picked up the receiver on the landline phone.

"Jazelle, we're here in the office now, if you'd like to bring the coffee," she said, then after a short pause added, "That would be nice. Jack might be getting hungry."

She hung up the phone just as he was easing onto the seat he'd placed next to hers.

"She'll be here shortly," she told him. "While we wait, I'll get the computer started."

"There's no need for you to hurry on my account," he told her.

Amused by his remark, she shot him an impish grin. "You look like my students right before test time. Don't worry. This isn't a test that you'll be scored on. It's more like a puzzle that you might be able to help solve."

"I hate to disappoint you, but I never was good at puzzles. When I was a kid, I always wanted to bend the ears on the pieces and make them fit, even if it was the wrong spot."

She chuckled. "A psychiatrist could tell you what that means about your personality. I can't. Other than it sounds like you were a naughty boy."

His grin was sheepish. "Only at times. I have a couple of brothers who were a lot peskier than me."

"Your mother must be made of iron," she joked.

She turned slightly away from him as she reached to open a drawer on the side of the desk, and Jack used the moment to let his gaze slide over her glossy black hair and the dress that draped off her bare shoulders. The red poppies on the fabric matched the red color of her lips, and Jack thought how she looked like an exotic flower.

"On the outside, Mom looks fragile. She's always been slender and delicate. But I guess she has a strong constitution. Otherwise, she couldn't have birthed and raised eight children. Plus, be a rancher's wife."

She lifted a stack of papers from the drawer and placed them on the desktop, before she turned a curious glance on him. "You make it sound like being a rancher's wife is a hard thing."

"Well, I'll put it this way. Being a rancher's wife on Stone Creek Ranch couldn't have been easy."

One corner of her lips curved upward, and Jack could hardly think as the urge to kiss her hit him like an avalanche.

"Why? Did your mother have to wash clothes at the creek?" she teased. "Or cook over an open fire?"

"Nothing so primitive. It's just that the ranch is isolated and far away from certain conveniences. Not to mention friends and entertainment."

Her blue eyes met his, and Jack felt sure something had jolted his chair. Did this area of Arizona experience tremors? he wondered. Or was something about looking into Vanessa's eyes altering his senses?

She said, "Sometimes a woman has other things to consider."

Like a roof over her head and food on the table? Or a fat bank account to buy whatever she pleased?

Or was she talking about a man to hold her in his arms? To make passionate love to her?

Thankfully, the questions running through his mind were interrupted by a light knock on the door, and he tore his gaze away from Vanessa's just in time to see the young housekeeper entering the room.

"Coffee and pastries have arrived," Jazelle said cheerfully. "Sorry, I'm running a bit late. Sophia drained the last of the coffee to take to Holt's office. I had to wait for another pot to finish brewing."

"We're in no hurry," Vanessa assured her. "Just put the tray on the table by the armchairs. I was just digging out the family tree I started making last week."

Jazelle put down the tray, then came over to stand in front of the desk where Vanessa and Jack were sitting. "Oh, I wish I had time to stay and help you two," she said as she twisted her head at an angle in order to see the upside-down papers. "I love trying to solve mysteries."

"It's more than a mystery, I'd say," Jack said.

His voice must have held a mocking note, because Jazelle arched a quizzical brow at him. "Oh. You don't believe you and the Hollisters are related?"

Did he? Before he'd arrived at Three Rivers Ranch, he would've bet everything in his bank account that he wasn't related to this group of people. But now a seed of uncertainty had sprouted in him and begun to grow.

"I wouldn't say I disbelieve it," he answered. "I just need to see some type of proof."

Smiling, Jazelle looked at Vanessa, then jerked her thumb in Jack's direction. "Look at him. What do you see?"

Chuckling, Jack momentarily covered his ears with his hands. "I might not want hear this."

"Well, I'll tell you," Jazelle went on before giving Vanessa time to answer the question. "I think Maureen is right. There's something about Jack that reminds me of Chandler and the late Mr. Hollister. I noticed it right off. What about you, Van?"

"I have noticed," Vanessa agreed. "But I also wonder if we're just seeing a resemblance because we expected to see one. Or maybe we even wanted to find a similarity in the men."

Tilting her head again, Jazelle gave Jack another long glance. "Hmm. Not all blue eyes are the same. Connor's eyes have that silvery color to them. Madison's are more like blue velvet. There's no wanting or expecting about it. Jack's eyes match Chandler's. But I have every faith in you, Van. In spite of who Jack does or doesn't resemble, you'll dig up the truth of the matter."

With a wave of her hand, Jazelle hurried out of the room, and after she'd shut the door behind her, Vanessa made a helpless, palms-up gesture. "Sorry, Jack. I'm sure you're getting tired of hearing this stuff."

"Actually, I'm beginning to find it amusing."

"And what if we discover you really are related to the Hollisters? Would that upset you?"

Frowning slightly, he shook his head. "I wouldn't say that. *Perplexed* would be more like it. But I'm positive that it wouldn't change me as a person."

She studied him for another long moment before she rose to her feet. "I'll get our coffee," she said as she walked over to the table where Jazelle had left the tray. "Do you want cream or sugar?"

Leaving his chair, Jack joined her at the table. "I take it plain."

"It wasn't necessary for you to get up," she told him. "I was going to bring it to you."

She started to reach for the insulated coffee urn, but Jack reached out and caught hold of her hand. The contact caused her gaze to sweep up to his face, and he didn't miss the surprise flickering in her eyes.

"I understand," he said. "But I wanted to say something to you before we got into the coffee or the research."

"Okay. I'm listening."

He drew in a deep breath and tried to ignore how soft her hand felt in his and how scant the space that separated their faces was.

"It's about last night. I—"

"If you're thinking you need to apologize for kissing me, I'm going to be damned disappointed," she said curtly. "So please, don't."

"I wasn't thinking you needed an apology," he told her. "I thought I should explain that I, uh, don't go around kissing women I've known for only a few hours. That's not my usual way of behaving."

The curve on her lips deepened, and as Jack stared at them, he remembered the exquisite taste, the pleasure that had flooded through him as he'd plundered the plump curves.

"And you think I go around kissing men I've just met?" she asked. "No. I don't. But then, none ever tried. Until you."

And he damned well wanted to be the last to try.

The possessive thought zinged through his head like a streak of lightning flashing across a cloudless sky. Now, where had that come from? He had no right or reason to think about laying claims on this woman.

"Well, I did admit that I was a naughty boy."

"You're a grown man now," she pointed out.

He slid his fingertips across the back of her hand and marveled at the smoothness of her skin. "Some things never change."

Her face inched ever so closer to his, and he wondered if she knew how hard and fast she was making his heart beat. Did she have any idea that the desire to kiss her was tying him into helpless knots?

"Thankfully. Some things never do change."

If Jack had any sense he'd start backpedaling and not stop until he was out in the hall and a safe distance away from her. But being close to her caused his common sense to short-circuit.

He was trying to think of a suitable reply and a

reason not to kiss her again when she decided to take the matter into her own hands and pressed her mouth to his.

The soft touch of her lips moving over his was like an incredible dream. If he had his way, he'd never open his eyes. Never wake from the pleasure rushing through him. But after a long, long moment, she ended the kiss just as abruptly as she'd started it.

Forcing his eyes open, Jack saw that her face had moved back from his but was still close enough to see the moisture of their kiss glistening on her lips and the tiny gold flecks circling the pupils of her eyes. Gazing at her was more potent than downing a double shot of bourbon, he thought. He felt drunk with the need to reach for her.

"What was that about?" he asked.

"I thought you deserved a proper greeting this morning. That's all."

"I'm not sure I need to see what you'd consider an improper greeting," he said half-jokingly.

She laughed lightly, and as she turned her attention to pouring the coffee, Jack noticed a tinge of pink color on her cheeks.

"There's something about you, Jack, that makes me act out of character. So just overlook my behavior toward you, will you?"

"If you're trying to tell me not to take you seriously, then don't worry. After all, a man and woman can enjoy a kiss without there being a special meaning behind it. Right?"

Something flashed in her eyes, and then a brief smile quirked her lips. "You are so right, Jack. There's nothing serious about a kiss between friends. It's just a pleasant exchange, nothing more."

Hell, who was he trying to kid? Her or himself? When his lips were wrapped over hers, he wasn't thinking of her as a friend. He was thinking of her as his lover. And unless he was reading her wrong, she was feeling the same way about him.

But none of that really mattered, he thought. It couldn't. Not with him going home to Utah in a few short days. And then all that would be left of this time with Vanessa would be memories.

Chapter Four

Rather than let Jack see the heat on her cheeks and the tremble in her hands, Vanessa turned away from him and began to fill two cups with steaming coffee.

Oh my! What was he really thinking? she wondered. Probably that she was behaving like a man-starved divorcée. And telling him that the kiss she'd given him was only a friendly greeting had to be lamest thing she'd ever said in her life. She'd kissed him like she was madly in love with him!

"You have to eat one of Reeva's cinnamon rolls," she told him, then hearing the husky tone in her voice, cleared her throat. "They're sinfully delicious."

"Sounds like I'd better try one," he said.

She placed one of the rolls and a fork onto a small plate, then handed it and one of the coffees to him.

While he carried his food and drink over to the desk, Vanessa served herself and tried to compose her rattled senses.

For the next few days, she'd be working closely with Jack, she reasoned with herself. She couldn't allow her attraction for him get out of hand. She'd be inviting huge heartache. Sure, he might enjoy kissing her. But he'd just made it perfectly clear that nothing about their little lip-lock was serious. And she'd be an idiot to believe he'd change his mind over the course of a few days.

She joined him at the desk, and he eyed the cup she placed on the ink pad in front of her.

"I don't see another cinnamon roll. Aren't you going to have one?" he asked.

She eased into the executive chair and wondered if he'd noticed if she inched it slightly away from him.

Of course he would notice, Vanessa! Why are you being such a ninny, anyway? You just initiated a kiss with the man, and now you're thinking you need to put space between the two of you. Don't you think it's a little late to distance yourself?

Trying to ignore the taunting voice in her head, she answered his question. "No. My breakfast is still with me. And while I'm living here on the ranch and working on the family tree, I'm trying not to over-indulge."

While he sipped his coffee, his gaze made a slow

survey of her face, and Vanessa had the silliest urge to smooth her hair and moisten her lips.

"How long do you plan on staying out here?" he asked.

"The answer to that question depends on you, I suppose. And what the two of us can come up with. If we can figure this ancestry thing out quickly, then Maureen won't need me. Not that she would tell me to go home," she added with a wry smile. "Neither she nor the others would mind if I stayed for several months."

"Would you like to stay here for several months? Or do you have…other interests in town?"

Was he talking about a man? The idea made her want to snort.

Staring at the milky coffee in her cup, she said, "I might stay on a bit longer. Being out here is like a vacation. As for my interest in town, the only one I have is my job at St. Francis. But I've taken a leave of absence until January."

"No boyfriend? Or special guy?"

She looked at him, while thinking they needed to quit all this personal talk and get on with the family tree. But she didn't have the heart to make the suggestion.

"No special guy," she said flatly. "I had one once, but he, uh, decided he didn't want to be hooked up with only me."

Her admission caused the fork he was holding to

pause over the cinnamon roll. "Was he a boyfriend? Fiancé?"

Clutching her coffee cup with both hands, she said, "You're getting personal now."

"I probably am," he conceded. "Because I'm curious. I'm having trouble figuring how a woman who looks like you can be unattached."

Funny, but she'd been asking herself the same question about him. "It's no secret, really. I was married once for a little while. Eight months to be exact."

His brows arched upward. "Eight months. You were just getting started. What happened? He died or was killed in an accident?"

Before Vanessa could stop it, a burst of laughter rushed out of her. Then, seeing her reaction had left a stunned look on his face, she shook her head.

"Sorry, Jack. I'm laughing because…well, it's hilarious to think that only death could have separated Steven from me. He missed that part of the marriage vows. Of course, I didn't know what kind of man he really was until it was too late and he was telling me he wanted a divorce. I think we'd been married about seven months at that time."

"Oh. You couldn't tell he was unstable?"

"Unstable?" Suddenly she was giggling uncontrollably. "He was about as steady as a ninety-year-old man walking a tightrope over Niagara Falls! And I believed he was the committed, forever kind. Is that not hilarious? Me, a teacher. I'm supposed to be smart."

He didn't say anything. Instead, he simply looked at her as though he was seeing her for the first time. The idea that he was likely summing her up as an idiot gave her the strength to stop the giggles, yet to her horror the untimely laughter was followed with a blur of tears.

Bending her head, she snatched up a napkin and dabbed at her eyes before the tears could spill onto her cheeks.

"Forgive me, Jack. I… I imagine you can tell I'm not used to talking about this to anyone. And it makes me angry at myself for getting emotional over the ordeal. It's not like I give a darn about the man anymore. We've been divorced for more than two years now. It's just…it's embarrassing to admit to being such a fool."

She sensed him leaning closer and then his hand clasped a gentle circle around her forearm. "You shouldn't beat yourself up about it, Vanessa," he said gently. "We all do foolish things at least one time in our lives. I believe it's called being human."

She blinked away the last of the moisture in her eyes, then lifting her head, she said, "Yes, but I don't suppose you've ever made such a stupid mistake."

His lips twisted into a cynical line. "You'd be wrong. Over the years, I've made some bad choices. But that's how we learn not to make the same mistakes, isn't it?"

She let out a rough breath as she nodded in agreement. "Yes. Life lessons. Sometimes they're hard."

He gave her arm a faint squeeze. "Sorry, Vanessa. I shouldn't have been asking you such personal things. It's none of my business."

Shaking back her hair, she bravely met his gaze. "Why not? I kissed you as if I had a right to. You should have the right to ask me a few personal questions."

After studying her for a long moment, he smiled. "You have a point there."

Relieved that the awkward moment had seemingly passed, she quickly went to work aligning four pieces of paper together on the desktop into a square.

"Here's what I've been working on this past week," she told him. "I thought using an actual family-tree diagram would make it easier for you and everyone to follow."

He leaned forward and peered earnestly at the names branched in all directions.

"As far as the Arizona Hollisters go, you already have a large number of names here," he said.

"Yes, the family have kept a few records of past generations, which made doing this easier for me. Now I need to begin working on your family," she said. "So a list of your family members would be helpful. Maureen has already given me a few names that Hadley gave her over the phone, but I'm thinking you might have more. Someone he's missed."

He tapped a long brown finger to the first entered descendants. "Is this as far back as you go?"

"For now it is. Until I can dig up more facts," she

answered. "Edmund and Helena came here from Virginia and established Three Rivers Ranch in 1847. The couple and their three children are all buried here on the ranch. I've not seen the graves myself, but I'm told they're located somewhere near the old cabin where the family first lived."

He didn't reply and she glanced over to see he was staring thoughtfully at the mountain view beyond the window. Was he thinking about these Hollisters? Or was something back home crowding in on his thoughts? Something personal that he didn't want to share with her?

Telling herself she didn't need to know that much about him, she asked, "Has your father or grandfather ever mentioned relatives from Virginia? Or any of your family settling in Arizona?"

He reached for his coffee. "Nothing remotely close," he replied. "I was just thinking how much history is in this ranch. How much work and dedication each generation must have put into it."

"I've thought a lot about that very thing. You don't see very much commitment and loyalty like that nowadays. Although, I'm discovering that not all the Hollister descendants in the past stuck around to be ranchers. Especially the women."

"I'm assuming they married and moved away," he said. "That was a woman's lot back then, wouldn't you say?"

"Mostly. Thankfully nowadays, public opinion of a woman who chooses to remain single has changed," she said. "It's much nicer to be labeled *strong and independent* rather than *undesirable*. But as for the Hollister women, they all married. Except for Edmund's daughter, Cynthia. Unfortunately, she died from diphtheria as a very young child, and then one son, George, died in a mining accident in 1872. Joseph, the surviving son, is the one who kept the Hollister name going."

His expression thoughtful, he sliced off a bite of cinnamon roll and ate it before he replied. "Looks like you have a good idea of how the family grew from there. Where does Maureen get the idea our family might be related?"

"That's where the mystery comes in, Jack. When Maureen first started this ancestry search, on several of the websites she was using, your father's name appeared as a possible relative. Especially when she tried to go back from Axel—that's Gil and Joel's dad. But she never could figure out why and, frankly, neither can I." She sipped her coffee and then reached for a notebook where she'd scribbled the scant information she had on the Utah Hollisters. "Do you know your paternal grandfather's name? I'll see if it matches what I found."

"Yes. It was Lionel Alford. He passed away a few years ago."

"That's what I have written down. I'm glad to know I've been on the right track." She picked up a pencil. "And his wife? I didn't find anything on her."

"Her name is Scarlett, and her maiden name was

Wilson. She and Grandfather divorced in the late '70s, and she pretty much left the family behind after that. We think she's still alive. At least, we've not heard any word of her passing."

"Oh, I'm sorry. Their breakup must have been a bitter one. Especially for her to leave a child behind. Did your father have siblings?"

"Two brothers. Wade and Barton." He took another bite of the sweet roll. "Neither was interested in ranching, and both of them moved away after they became adults."

She hurriedly scribbled down what he'd just told her. "Does your father keep in touch with them?"

"Not much. As far as I know there never was any ill will between them. The way I see it, the brothers never had any common interests. And once they moved away, I guess you could say they all drifted apart."

She underlined the two men's names. "How sad. I'd hate to think my brother didn't care whether he saw me or talked to me. Siblings are a blessing."

He took a sip of coffee before he glanced at her. "I'll tell you, Vanessa, ever since Dad told the family about the ancestry mystery, I've been trying to think how these Hollisters on Three Rivers could be connected with my dad and uncles. If it's true that there is a connection, it would have to be in the distant past. Before Dad and his brothers were even born. Wouldn't that have to be the case?"

"Logically, yes. And I've been trying to come up

with a scenario in which it could have happened. I even ran the idea of Axel having a secret baby with a woman in Utah. He could've gone up there to buy cattle or horses and ended up, uh, having a brief tryst."

His expression thoughtful, he drummed his fingers against the desktop. "Unless my grandmother, Scarlett, somehow got involved with Axel and she ultimately passed the baby off as belonging to her husband, Lionel. That's a far-fetched notion, but not completely impossible."

Intrigued by the possibility, Vanessa said, "That would mean your father or one of his brothers would be Gil's half brother. Wow! Do you believe your grandmother could've done such a thing?"

"Since I never actually knew her, it would be just an assumption on my part. Dad rarely mentions the woman, and when he does it's not in a favorable light. But when you think about it, Scarlett left her sons behind. Not just for a short while but indefinitely. Having an illicit affair couldn't have been any worse."

"Hmm. Perhaps that was one of the reasons your grandparents divorced. Because she was involved with another man."

He frowned and shrugged. "Dad has never talked much about his parents' relationship. I imagine it's an unpleasant subject for him. I'm not sure he even knows why they divorced. At that time he and his brothers were young. Dad was probably around eighteen."

Vanessa slanted him an empathetic look. "Well, it's just one scenario, anyway. Besides, we might discover there's really no connection between the two Hollister families and that the whole idea was the product of a glitch in the system. Meanwhile, I'm going to do a search on your uncles and see if that generates any results."

"For your sake, I hope it does."

She smiled. "My sake? I don't have a dog in this hunt."

"No. But you're the one doing all the hunting."

"I'm enjoying the challenge." Especially now that he was here, she thought. He'd been around less than twenty-four hours, yet his presence had already made a mark on her.

Actually, when Maureen had first mentioned to Vanessa that Jack was traveling down to Three Rivers, Vanessa had told her it was unnecessary. She could get all the information she needed from him over the phone. But Maureen had told her that meeting a person face-to-face could tell her much more than a phone conversation. And now she was seeing just how right Maureen had been.

"Good thing. You might have a very long challenge," he said, then asked, "Is there anything else you need to know about my family? If you'd like them just for record, I can write down the names of my siblings and their birthdays."

"Thanks. That would be a help. And I need your paternal great-grandfather's name. That would be

Lionel's dad. Is he the one who established your family ranch?"

Shaking his head, he said, "No. Lionel began building Stone Creek Ranch around 1960, I think. As for his father, I believe his name was Peter Hollister. Grandfather rarely talked about the man, so there's not much I can tell you. Except that he died way back in the early 1940s when Grandfather was only a toddler. But from what we understand, Peter was from Utah and lived around the area where we live now. Supposedly that's why Lionel settled there."

"I see. And what about his wife? I'm assuming she's probably deceased by now," she said as she quickly wrote the details he'd given her in the notebook.

"Great-grandmother's name was Audrey. From what Dad says, she died at a very early age, also."

"This is all helpful, Jack. You've given me something to work with."

He said, "I talked to my father earlier this morning, and he's champing at the bit to hear what you've come up with so far."

She arched her brows at him. "Oh, dear. And I'm just getting started. Your father must be an impatient man."

He chuckled. "Aren't all men impatient?"

Laughing softly, she said, "I'd better not answer that. I'd like us to remain friends."

"You needn't worry about that, Vanessa. I think we're going to be great friends."

Buddies. Pals. Two people who merely liked each other. That was all the two of them could be, Vanessa told herself. But as her eyes feasted on his rugged features and her mind relived the pleasure of his kiss, she couldn't help but wish they could be far more than friends.

She pressed the Power button on the computer and hoped he couldn't read her thoughts.

"I'm glad, Jack. Hopefully, I can come up with some answers for you to take back to Utah."

"Back to Utah," he repeated thoughtfully. "Well, I'll tell you, Vanessa, right now I'm going to enjoy my time here on Three Rivers."

She looked at him and smiled. "I'm going to enjoy my time here, too."

Until Jack said goodbye, she thought. And then she'd be left to wonder *what if.* What if she'd been brave enough to let herself get close to him? Brave enough to experience real passion? Even for only a few days?

Later that night after dinner, Jack was in the den having a casual conversation with Blake and Taggart O'Brien, the ranch foreman, when Maureen and Gil entered the room and took up seats directly across from the three men.

"What is this?" Gil asked jokingly. "Maureen and I walk up and suddenly you guys go quiet."

Taggart chuckled. "When the boss shows up, it's best to be quiet."

Jack looked questioningly at the foreman. "Which one is the boss?"

Laughing heartily, Gil jerked a thumb at Maureen. "She is, of course."

Glancing at Blake, Jack asked, "Is that true? Maureen is the boss around here?"

"It's absolutely the truth," Blake answered. "Gil will tell you that we're just Mom's underlings."

Her smile wide, Maureen shook her head. "Don't pay any attention to them, Jack. We're all in this together. Although, I confess I am a bit bossy."

They all laughed at this, and then Blake said, "I thought you two were going to drive over to the Reynolds' ranch this evening. What happened? He backed out on selling the bull?"

"Hugh didn't back out. An appointment came up in town tonight that he couldn't put off," Gil answered. "Which worked out okay with your mother and me because we have something we wanted to discuss with Jack."

Jack's attention went on sudden alert. What could they possibly want to discuss that couldn't have been said over the dinner table? Had Vanessa found pertinent information to tie the two families together? If so, Jack couldn't imagine Maureen and Gil keeping a lid on such news until now. As for Vanessa, he'd left the study shortly before noon and had spent most of the afternoon with Taggart.

Telling himself that now wasn't the time to be thinking about Vanessa or her kisses, Jack glanced around to see Blake had arched his brows with curiosity. Next to him, Taggart rose to his feet.

"I need to be leaving. It'll take me thirty minutes to get Emily-Ann and Brody away from the playroom," the foreman said, then directed a wry glance at Jack. "If you accidently wander onto the third floor, beware of the last door on the east end of the house or you might be run over by stampeding kids."

Chuckles rippled through the group as Maureen said, "Tag, there's no need for you to rush off. What we have to say to Jack can be said in front of you. You're family, too. Besides, it won't hurt to let Brody play with the kids for a few more minutes."

Jack had already noticed how these Hollisters treated their employees like relatives, especially Taggart, Luke, Colt and Jim. As much as Jack could recall, the five ranch hands who worked for Stone Creek rarely entered the house and had never joined them at the dinner table. Maybe that was a situation that needed to change, he thought.

Maureen waited for Taggart to return to his seat before she directed her attention to Jack.

"We've been talking with Van," she said. "And it seems as though she's bogged down with the family search. Some of the names you gave her this morning are drawing a complete blank."

He'd expected to see Vanessa whenever the family gathered in the den for drinks, but she'd not appeared for cocktails or for dinner. Although her absence had left him wondering, he hadn't asked anyone of her whereabouts. He hadn't wanted to appear *that* obvious. Still, his thoughts had been preoccupied with her and whether she might be trying to avoid him. By why would she? Was she afraid they might end up sharing another kiss?

Telling himself to forget about Vanessa, Jack reacted to Maureen's news with a cynical laugh. "Must have been some aliases and outlaws in our family."

Maureen and Gil exchanged amused glances.

"I wouldn't assume that," Gil said. "There could be a number of reasons she can't find a trace of them."

Jack said, "I honestly have no idea why they can't be found. Unless the names could have different spellings. It would probably help if I had addresses or phone numbers, but Dad and his brothers don't really keep in touch. Most likely any information he has for them isn't current."

Gil batted a dismissive hand through the air. "Don't worry, Jack. Addresses and phone numbers aren't that hard to come by. Maureen and I have something else in mind."

Jack watched the older couple exchange knowing glances, before Maureen said, "We do have something else in mind. The last time I spoke with Hadley on the phone, he said something that made lots of sense."

Jack grunted with amusement. "I hope he was doing it without yelling or cursing."

Maureen smiled. "Your father has been a complete gentleman. Gil and I are looking forward to meeting him. No matter the outcome of this family-tie thing. But he suggested that we need something concrete to go on before we really throw ourselves into a serious search."

"That's well and good, Mom," Blake spoke up. "But where is the concrete evidence going to come from? Do you know of any more archived family papers we have around here? Something that might give us a few clues?"

"I'm not sure if there's anything left in the attic or not. I'm going to check on that tomorrow. What Gil and I are thinking is a DNA test." She leveled a serious look at Jack. "Would you be willing to have your DNA compared to ours?"

All sorts of thoughts and questions raced through Jack's mind as he stared at Maureen, then moved his gaze to the men nearby. And from reading the expressions on their faces, they were all waiting expectantly for him to answer.

"To be honest, the idea of a DNA test did run through my mind before I ever started the drive down here to Arizona."

"Oh. Have you already mentioned to your father the possibility of doing one?" Gil asked.

Jack shook his head. "No. We didn't discuss the idea. I think he believes we can figure it out just by searching through ancestry sites."

"Let's hope we can," Maureen said. "Because if by some chance your DNA did match Gil's or my children's, we'd still have the question of how the relation occurred."

"That's true," Blake agreed. "Just saying our genes matched wouldn't be enough."

Nodding, Jack replied, "On the other hand, if it turned out we're not related, there would be no need to continue with the hunt."

"Does that mean you're agreeable to the idea?" Maureen asked.

"Sure. Why not? I can't see that it would hurt anything one way or the other," Jack told her. "At least it would answer the main question."

Smiling with relief, Maureen clapped her hands together. "This is wonderful, Jack. You're being a real sport about this."

Taggart was the next person to speak. "So who's going to be your family's donor, Maureen?"

She leveled a pointed look at Blake. "I thought you'd make a good specimen, Blake."

"Ha! Mom, all of your children have the same DNA. And come to think of it, Joe will probably be on duty at the sheriff's office. He and Jack can do the test right there."

"And when Jack arrives at the sheriff's office, Joe could be called out on an emergency," Maureen reasoned. "Blake, I'd really like for you to be with Jack when the test is done. For moral support. Not that a swab is anything to dread, but the idea of getting your self-identity inspected might be a little unnerving to the both of you."

Blake glanced at Jack and chuckled. "I guess she means two ranch managers together are better than one in any situation."

"Of course you two are better together." She quickly rose from the love seat and headed to the bar. "I think this calls for a toast, don't you, Gil?"

The elder Hollister followed his wife. "I certainly do. I'll get the glasses while you find something nice for us to sip on—like the expensive bourbon Jazelle keeps hidden for Holt. He'll never know we got into it."

"What won't I know? Mom, are you digging into my whiskey?"

At the sound of Holt's voice, Jack looked around to see the horse trainer and his veterinarian brother entering the room through the French doors. Both men looked dirty and tired, and as they came farther into the room, each one removed his dusty hat and swatted it against the side of his leg.

"Well, well. It's pretty common to see Chandler dragging in with the dry cows," Blake commented. "But what are you doing here so late, Holt?"

"Chandler has been helping me treat a cut on a mare's leg," Holt explained as he and Chandler sank into a pair of empty wing chairs.

"Jim or Colt couldn't take care of the mare?" Taggart asked.

"Probably," Chandler spoke up with a weary grin. "But Holt wanted a professional on the job. He's a mother hen when it comes to Doll Brown."

Blake rolled his eyes while Taggart chuckled.

From across the wide room, Gil explained to the two men, "Your mother and I are getting some drinks for a toast. Would you two like to join us?"

"Sure. What are we toasting?" Holt turned an anxious look on Blake. "If Kat's had the twins, what are you doing here?"

Blake laughed. "Kat is upstairs resting. No labor pains yet."

"Oh, heck!" Holt exclaimed with obvious disappointment. "When are those little fellas going to make their entrance?"

"Who says they're going to be boys?" Maureen asked from her position behind the bar.

Holt chuckled smugly. "Remember, Mom, I'm an expert on predicting the sex of babies."

"Yes, equine babies," Blake reminded him. "There is a difference."

"Not really," Holt said as he raked a weary hand over his thick hair. "They're both magnificent."

The veterinarian glanced around the den. "Speaking of Kat and women, where are all the moms and kids? Jack's going to start getting the impression we keep our offspring hidden away."

Blake laughed. "No, we keep them contained. Like a herd of cattle."

"Oh, Blake, please," Maureen said with a playful groan, then to answer Chandler's question, she added, "They're all upstairs."

"So what are we toasting?" Holt asked again.

"Jack and Blake are going to get DNA tests to see if the two families are a match," Gil said as he dropped ice cubes into squat tumblers.

From the corner of his eye, Jack noticed Holt and Chandler exchanging pointed glances.

"What's wrong?" Jack asked the two men. "Do you think doing the test is a mistake? Or are you worried my father has thoughts of getting hands on your money or assets?"

"Hell, Jack, we're not thinking your family is up to anything sinister," Holt quickly assured him. "After all, Mom is the one who started this whole thing. Not you Utah Hollisters."

"I think Holt and I are just thinking how weird it all seems to look at you and think you might possibly be kin," Chandler told Jack. "And I imagine you're looking at us and thinking the same thing."

"The idea still seems fantastic to me," Jack admitted.

"Which is a good reason to do the test," Blake said. "One way or the other, we'll know. And then we can all quit wondering about that aspect of the mystery."

Gil carried the tray of drinks over to the group of men and passed them around. After everyone had a tumbler in hand, he turned to his wife.

"Do you want to make the toast?" he asked.

Standing close to his side, Maureen wrapped an arm against the back of his waist and with her free hand lifted her glass high.

"You're the eldest Hollister here," she told her husband. "This is your legacy."

Gil was Maureen's second husband and brother to her late first husband, Joel. Which made him very much a part of the Hollister name and legacy.

"Our name—this ranch—the heritage belongs to all of us." Gil lifted his glass and clinked it against Maureen's. "Here's to the truth."

And what might the truth turn out to be? Jack wondered. That someone in one of the Hollister families had had a back-street affair? That a son was born and later shunned because of his illicit conception? As far as he was concerned, the truth could end up hurting people.

But who was he trying to kid? This growing preoccupation he had with Vanessa could end up hurting him far more than learning one of his relatives had been a rogue or worse.

Chapter Five

Vanessa closed her eyes and used her fingertips to lightly massage the burning lids. There was no point in continuing the search for information on Peter Hollister tonight. She wasn't making any progress, and after spending all evening helping corral the twins for Katherine, she needed a break.

You need more than a break, Vanessa. You need to purge your mind completely of Jack Hollister. A few days with him could turn into a lifetime of heartache.

Doing her best to ignore the cynical voice in her head, she shut off the computer and desk lamp, then made her way out of the dark study.

At this late hour she was expecting everyone to

have already retired to their rooms for the night. When she spotted Jack down the hallway, she watched in surprise as he passed the staircase and continued toward her.

Closing the study door behind her, she stood in place until he reached her.

"You're up late tonight," she remarked.

"I could say the same thing about you." He gestured toward the door behind her. "You weren't at dinner. Don't tell me you've been working on the family tree all this time."

Had he missed her? she wondered, then silently laughed at that idea. Jack wasn't the type of man to pine for a woman's company. No. She figured he was the sort who could easily do without a woman's chatter—or kiss.

"No. I've only been here in the study for about thirty minutes."

"Oh. Well, when you didn't show up for drinks or dinner I thought you might have gone into town for…something."

He was wearing a pale blue shirt that matched his eyes, and Vanessa was finding it difficult not to stare at him. "I don't need anything in town—yet," she told him. "I've been helping Tallulah watch Abby and Andy. These days the nanny is staying longer than usual in the evenings to give Kat a chance to rest. The twins could arrive any moment, and she's pretty drained right now."

"Blake seems like the kind of husband and father who'd be there to help his wife."

"He's very good about helping Kat. But she knows how hard Blake works. She wants him to have a little downtime, too."

Nodding that he understood the situation, he said, "That's nice of you to give Tallulah a hand. But I missed you."

His unexpected remark jolted her, but she tried her best to make light of it. After all, she figured he was only making polite conversation.

"I'm sure the Hollisters kept you entertained."

"Not the way you would have."

Was he referring to the kiss she'd plastered on his lips this morning? The idea sent a wash of heat over her face, and she hoped the footlights in the hallway were too dim for him to notice she was blushing.

She cleared her throat. "Um, what are you doing up so late?"

"Talking with the Hollisters," he said. "Were you on your way to your room?"

"No. Actually, I was going to the kitchen to see if there was any dessert left over from dinner. Jazelle brought slices of cake up to the playroom for the kids, but I missed getting any."

"I didn't eat dessert. Maybe my share will be there," he suggested with a grin.

"Why don't you join me? We can have a snack together."

"Sounds good," he told her. "I'm too wide awake to go to bed, anyway."

Walking side by side, the two of them made their way through the quiet house until they reached the kitchen. A small night-light over the counter cast enough light to show Vanessa the way to a built-in booth situated on the same wall as the stove.

She switched on a lamp hanging over the wooden table and gestured to one of the benches.

"Have a seat, and I'll get the cake. The coffee is all gone, but if you'd like a cup, I can make some."

"Thanks, but no. The cake will be plenty."

He made himself comfortable on one side of the booth, and she went in search of dessert. To her delight there was plenty stored away in the refrigerator, and she cut two ample pieces and placed them on paper plates to save dirtying the china.

She joined him at the booth and placed one of the servings along with a fork in front of him. "I hope you don't mind eating off paper."

"Not at all," he said. "My family isn't the fine-china sort. What about yours?"

She chuckled as she sat down across from him. "Mom always wanted her dishes to be the hard plastic kind. Otherwise, my sister and I were constantly breaking them. Especially when we had kitchen-cleaning duty. Actually, Mom still uses the plastic. Unless she and Dad have special guests over. Which isn't often. They don't socialize all that much. What about your parents? Do they have many guests and parties like they do here at Three Rivers?"

"Not often. And when they do have a get-together it's nothing fancy." He picked up the fork she'd given him and sliced off a bite of the chocolate confection. "See, we're nothing like these Hollisters. Except that we both have big families, and we ranch for a living. However, Blake tells me they have other holdings that bring in money. Like mining shares and things of that sort."

"Investing wisely and years of hard work. Yes, it's paid off for this family. But money isn't everything. I'm sure any of these Hollisters would tell you that their loved ones mean more than anything else."

He glanced over at her, and Vanessa wondered why it felt as though she'd known him for a long time. Why did she feel so connected to him? Just because she knew how his lips tasted? How it felt to have his arms wrapped around her?

No. No, Vanessa. Don't be thinking about those things now. You need to be thinking ahead to the day this man will drive away from Three Rivers Ranch.

"You know, after what you told me about your divorce, I'm surprised you've managed to stay a romantic," he said.

Her heart thumped erratically as she deliberately dropped her gaze from his face. "I didn't realize I was a romantic."

He reached across the table and slid a forefinger across the back of her hand. "You showed me the

North Star hanging over the desert. Don't you think that's a little romantic?"

He was flirting with her, and she couldn't begin to guess why. "Could be that I simply like astronomy."

"Could be."

She forced her gaze to return to his face. "My mother says that the divorce has left me jaded. And maybe it did in the beginning. But I've tried not to let it twist my thinking. If I allowed the ordeal with Steven to shape my future, I'd be quashing every wish I'd ever had for myself."

His gaze connected with hers, and something fluttered ever so softly in the middle of her chest.

"And those wishes would be…?" he asked.

He'd already summed her up as a hopeless romantic. There wasn't any purpose in pretending she wanted to spend the rest of her life as a single, independent woman. Yes, when her very short marriage had ended, she'd doubted she'd ever want to try again. But gradually she'd come to realize she couldn't let one mistake ruin her dreams.

"To have a family of my own. A husband and children." She shrugged. "Some women are perfectly fine with throwing all their focus into a career, and if that makes them happy, I say good for them. But that's not me. Yes, I love my job, but I need more than just the classroom."

"Well, it's good that you know what you want in life."

She gave him a vague smile. "Knowing what you want is three-fourths of the way to reaching your goals. Or so I've heard."

He turned his attention back to the cake. "I think you should know that Blake and I are going up to Prescott tomorrow to have a DNA swab taken."

She stared at him in wonder. "Really? Who suggested this?"

"Maureen and Gil. But actually, I had already tossed around the idea. It's the concrete evidence we need. So I figure it's the right thing to do."

"Hmm. Yes, it would help solve the main issue of whether there really is a connection. Have you told your family about this plan?"

"I had just gotten off the phone with Dad when I saw you in the hallway. He's agreeable. In fact, he was downright pleased. He wants this thing to be over and for me to get home."

Home. Yes, one way or the other, Jack would be leaving. There wouldn't be a chance for any more stargazing, late-night desserts or unplanned kisses.

Stifling a sigh, she tried to smile. "I'm sure he's missing his right-hand man—or son, I should say."

With a slight shake of his head, he said, "I wouldn't say I'm any more of a right-hand man to Dad than my brother Cordell. We call him Cord. He's the foreman of Stone Creek Ranch."

"Like Tag is the foreman for Three Rivers?"

"Yes. But Cord's job is on a much smaller scale than Tag's. Cord keeps the hands in line and doing what they're supposed to be doing. And he makes sure the cattle and sheep are where they should be and have everything they need. Especially in the winter months."

"Do you have much cold and snow where you live?"

"Yes. And we have to be prepared for the bad weather before it hits. And that includes making sure all the sheep and cattle are moved down from the higher altitudes."

She could easily imagine Jack working outdoors on horseback, swinging a lariat and herding cattle. Yet whenever it came to picturing him with a girlfriend, her mind turned to nothing but fog. She supposed that was because subconsciously she didn't want to envision him with a woman. Which was ridiculous. She had no right to be jealous over Jack.

Shoveling up the last bite of cake on her plate, she decided to move away from the subject of him returning to Utah. Instead, she asked, "So back to the DNA test, where are you planning to have it performed? Couldn't they do it in Wickenburg at the hospital or health department?"

"Possibly. I don't know. Since Joseph works in the sheriff's office for Yavapai County, we're going there to have it done."

"Oh, I hadn't thought about Joe and the sheriff's office. That will be good. You can rest assured that nothing could be tampered with."

He grunted with amusement. "Who knows, I

might find out I match up with a criminal in the sheriff's data system," he said jokingly.

"Are you worried, Jack? About the outcome, I mean."

"Not really," he answered, then shrugged. "It's not like it's something I can change."

She leaned back in the booth. "I imagine Maureen told you I'm having problems with your great-grandfather's name."

"Yes, she did. Is that why you'd gone back to the study this evening to work on him?"

"One reason. I'm not finding a Peter Hollister," Vanessa told him. "Not one that would match you or your family."

"What about my grandfather Lionel? If you could find something on him, then you could work back and possibly uncover information on Peter."

"I found Lionel Hollister with a prior address in your area, but no pertinent information like his birthdate or where he was born. It's weird."

"It's downright spooky," he agreed. "So what now?"

"Like I said before, Jack, I'm just beginning. In the morning I'm going to try a different ancestry site. So far the software I've been using is fairly simple. I'm going to move to a more sophisticated one that will hopefully dig deeper. Don't worry. There are more angles we can take to get results. And it could be something as simple as the spelling. Believe it or not, there's many ways the name can be spelled."

"Well, I was joking a moment ago about me matching a criminal. But sometimes I do wonder about my great-grandfather. His existence has always been surrounded by mystery. Like no one knew much about him, or if they did they didn't want to tell it."

"Hmm. Almost all families have a black sheep of sort. I'm trying hard not to be ours."

He arched a brow at her. "You're joking now, right?"

She let out a light laugh. "Yes, I'm joking," she admitted, then gestured to his empty plate. "Would you like more cake? There's plenty left in the fridge."

"No, thanks. I should be getting to my room. Blake wants to get an early start in the morning so he can get back here by noon for an appointment."

"I'll go up with you," she told him. "It's time I went to bed, too."

After dealing with their dirty plates and forks, Vanessa switched off the light over the booth, and they made their way back through the house and down the hall to the staircase.

As they climbed each step together, Jack said, "Our house on Stone Creek has two stories, and my bedroom faces the north and a ridge of distant mountains. Funny how I didn't think much about it until I came here. Three Rivers is beautiful, and everything about the house is incredibly comfortable. But a few times I've caught myself missing home."

"I hate to hear that. I was hoping you liked it here," she replied.

"I do like it. But home is—"

"Where the heart is," she finished for him, while wondering if he ever invited a woman out to his family's ranch. Unlike her, he hadn't blabbed about his personal life. A fact that only made her more curious.

He said, "Yes. Something like that."

"Do all your siblings live in the house?"

"No. Hunter has a separate house of his own on the property. Since he's on the road traveling with the rodeo company so much, it works better that way. And Grace lives in Beaver. That's where her medical practice is located."

She glanced at him. "So that leaves six of you. And your parents."

He slanted her an amused look. "And you're wondering how that many people exist in a house far smaller than this one."

"Well, I was thinking you'd have to be close."

"Like packed sardines? Not really. The house is actually spacious," he said with a chuckle. "And for the past few years Dad has made plans to build more rooms onto the house, but we—us kids—told him not to bother with the expense. Eventually, we all plan to move out and build places of our own. But for now the twins share a room. Cord and I have separate rooms. But Flint and Quint share a room, so it works out fairly well. Until the twins start fussing over who has first dibs on their bathroom and Quint gripes about Flint coming in at all hours of the night."

"And what about you and Cord? Which one of you two brothers comes in late at night?" she asked with a suggestive grin.

He grimaced. "Not me. Cord is the big socializer. There probably aren't many women left in Beaver County that he hasn't dated."

"Wow! Must be sparsely populated," she commented.

He laughed under his breath. "You don't know Cord."

She didn't know Jack, either. But she wanted to, Vanessa thought. She wanted to learn every little thing about him. That way, once he was gone, she'd have more to remember. Which was probably a masochistic idea, she admitted to herself. Because remembering this time with Jack would no doubt bring on sad feelings of loss.

On the second floor they walked to the end of the balcony and stopped in front of Vanessa's door. As they stood together in the semidarkness, her heightened senses were registering the quietness of the house, the closeness of his body and the unique scent of him drifting to her nostrils. She desperately wanted to slip her arms around his lean waist and angle her mouth up to his. But she'd already invited him to kiss her before. It was high time she kept her urges to herself.

"Here you are," he murmured. "Safely delivered to your bedroom door."

"Thanks for the company, Jack."

He didn't reply. Instead, his hand wrapped around hers, and he lifted the back of it to his lips. The sweet contact caused something in the middle of her chest to squeeze, and poignant tears to sting the backs of her eyes.

"It's been my pleasure, Vanessa."

He folded her hand between the two of his, and all she could think was how much she would like to feel his rough palms sliding over her skin, cupping her breasts, her face and every other place that was aching for his touch.

"Well, I…guess I should say good-night."

His hands tightened ever so slightly around hers. "I should say good-night, too. But I'm not sure I want to end this time with you just yet."

Her heart was suddenly tripping over itself. "Just how much time do you think you'll need?"

His chuckle fanned her cheeks, and then he was whispering, "Long enough to do…this."

As his lips settled over hers, desire shot through her, and forward or not, she didn't hesitate to respond with all that she was feeling.

In a matter of seconds, she felt his arms wrapping around her shoulders, drawing her to his chest. At the same time, his tongue was pushing against her teeth, begging for the invitation to slip inside.

As soon as she gave him complete access, he

thrust his tongue deep into her mouth, where it explored the ridges along the roof and the sharp edges of her teeth. The erotic sensation caused her to groan deep in her throat and circle her arms around his waist.

Was it possible for a person to melt from a kiss? Or was she simply going to fly off into space? Vanessa was asking herself those things when Jack's mouth eased slightly from hers, and as his lips hovered over hers, he whispered, "I never knew a kiss could taste like yours, Vanessa. It's like exotic fruit. Sweet and tart at the same time. And I could kiss you for hours."

"Hours?" she whispered in a drowsy voice. "I think I'd like that—very much."

This time when his lips came down on hers, she wasn't thinking about showing restraint. Instead, she tightened the hold she had on his waist and met his searching kiss with equal hunger.

On and on the kiss continued until Vanessa's whole body felt as though it was morphing into a giant flame that was on the verge of consuming both of them. But as the pleasure of his lips continued to send shock waves of pleasure through her body, she could only think it didn't matter if she turned to ashes. At least she'd be perishing in his arms.

She was clutching handfuls of the back of his shirt and hoping her knees would continue to hold her upright when somewhere in the house she heard a door opening and closing.

The sound caused her to stiffen, and he promptly lifted his head and squinted to the opposite side of the balcony.

"Did I hear a door?" he asked in a hushed voice.

She sucked in a deep breath and shoved her tousled hair off her face as she attempted to compose herself. "I think so. Apparently we, uh, aren't the only ones who are still up."

"Guess not." His breathing still a bit ragged, he glanced ruefully at her. "And maybe that's a good thing. We were getting a little lost, don't you think?"

She'd been lost, all right. Even now she wasn't sure her feet were solidly on the floor. "I'm…afraid you're right."

"Afraid?"

Her gaze searched through the shadows to find his. "Well, we shouldn't be—" She searched for words that would sound logical. But how could she come up with the right words when nothing about her reaction to Jack was logical?

"Acting like a man and woman attracted to each other?" he asked quietly. "Is that what you're thinking?"

"Not exactly," she said, then realizing she was still holding on to the back of his shirt, she allowed her hands to drop. "I'm thinking it wouldn't be good to let myself start liking you too much. Not with you going home to Utah in a few days."

He let out a long breath. "No. It wouldn't do for me to get to liking you too much, either. Maybe we ought to put a stop to this kissing stuff. Just play it safe and keep things friendly."

He was making all kinds of good sense, so why was his suggestion turning her insides to cold stone?

Bending her head so that he couldn't see the disappointment in her eyes, she said, "That's probably the smartest thing we could do."

"Be smart. Yeah, that's the best course."

Lifting her head, she gave him a wobbly smile. "We'll still be friends."

"Sure." He gently touched his fingertips to her cheeks. "Good night, Vanessa."

For one wild second, the idea of grabbing his hand and tugging him into her room dashed through her head, but just as quickly she shook the urge away.

"Good night, Jack. I'll see you tomorrow."

Turning, she entered her bedroom and locked the door behind her. But later, as she climbed into bed and turned off the light, she knew a lock on a door wasn't nearly enough to keep Jack out of her mind or her heart.

The next morning, Jack glanced at the clock on the dashboard of Blake's truck as he parked in the graveled area behind the big ranch house.

"Looks like we made it back from Prescott in time for your meeting," Jack said.

The two men had left early this morning for the ninety-minute drive to the Yavapai County sheriff's office for the DNA test. Once there, they'd had to wait for someone to perform the swab and do all the necessary paperwork. But for the most part everything had gone smoothly. Now it was just a matter of waiting for the results.

"Yeah. I have about thirty minutes to spare, so I'm going to go check on Kat before I head to the ranch yard," Blake told him as the two men exited the cab of the truck. "She wasn't feeling all that great this morning."

"I was about twelve when Mom was pregnant with my twin sisters. I remember her keeping her feet propped up on a cushion and eating peanut butter straight out of the jar. I thought her belly was going to pop."

Blake chuckled. "Kat says hers feels like it can't stretch another half inch."

They walked across the yard, past the patio and onto the small porch that led into the kitchen. Blake opened the door, then paused and looked over at Jack.

"Before we go in and everyone starts tossing questions at us, I just want to say thanks, Jack."

"No thanks are necessary."

"Maybe not. But like Holt said last night, Mom instigated the whole ancestry thing. And to be frank, we've all gone along with her because she's… Well, I'm sure in what little time you've been here, you can see for yourself that she's very special to us. And we like to make her happy, if it's in our power to do so."

Jack thought how nice it would be if he and his siblings considered their mother's feelings to the same extent as these Hollisters. True, all of Claire's children loved her, but sometimes they were too busy with their own lives to concern themselves with hers.

Jack said, "I understand. Look, Blake, I'm in the same boat with Dad about this ancestry thing. I don't want to disappoint him, either. So we had our mouths swabbed. It's the least we can do to make our parents happy."

Blake slapped a hand on Jack's shoulder and gave it a grateful shake. "Come on, let's go in. Reeva and Sophia should be getting lunch ready. If I'm lucky I might have time to eat before the cattle buyer arrives."

Inside the house, the two men washed up at the mudroom sink, then stepped into the busy kitchen and were promptly greeted with the smells of just-baked pizza and happy squeals from a table full of children.

"Daddy! Daddy!" Both twins shouted the moment they spotted their father walking into the room.

"Come eat with us, Daddy!" Andrew called out.

"We're having pizza with mushrooms on top," Abagail added, as though that was a special treat. "It's yummy, Daddy! You'll like it!"

Jack watched the ranch manager move across the room to where the twins were sitting with Chandler's two children and Jazelle's son and daughter.

Tallulah, the nanny, was seated with them, but Vanessa was nowhere in sight, and he wondered if she'd already eaten lunch.

"Sit at the booth, Jack. It's quieter," Reeva, the older cook, said as she tended something cooking in a big iron skillet. "Sophia will get you a plate."

He was opening his mouth to tell Reeva he wasn't all that hungry when from the corner of his eye he spotted Vanessa entering the kitchen through the swinging doors on the opposite side of the room.

"Thanks, Reeva. I'll, uh, see if Vanessa wants to join me."

He went to the middle of the room to intercept her and was relieved when she greeted him with a smile. Perhaps the things he'd said to her last night hadn't made her angry. Perhaps she understood the situation he was trying to avoid, even more than he understood it himself.

"I see you and Blake made it back from Prescott," she said. "How did the test go?"

Looking at her face was a feast for his eyes, he thought. Her skin was as smooth as satin, and the rich color of her blue eyes was warm and enticing. But it was the plump curves of her lips that wreaked havoc with his common sense. Even now, with the room full of people, he wanted to bend his head down to hers and taste them. How in hell was he ever going to stick to their friendship pact?

"No problems," he answered. "Now it's just a wait-and-see thing."

"In other words, now comes the hard part."

"I'm afraid you're right," he told her.

Behind him, he could hear Blake assuring the children he'd be back to eat with them as soon as he checked on their mother. Jack could only wonder what it would be like to have small children hugging his neck, kissing his cheek and begging him for his attention. Moreover, how would it feel to have a wife who needed and wanted his love and support? A woman like Vanessa to warm his empty bed and fill the vacant spots in his life?

"Have you eaten lunch yet?" she asked.

"No. Actually, we just walked in."

"Except for a slice of toast and a cup of coffee, I haven't had anything since I got out of bed this morning," she told him. "The smell of the pizza lured me to the kitchen."

"Hey, you two," Sophia called to them as she placed two tall glasses filled with ice on the booth table. "Your lunch is waiting."

"I believe she's expecting the two of us to eat together," Jack told Vanessa. "Is that okay with you?"

As if he needed more assurance, she grabbed his hand and urged him over to the built-in booth.

While they took their seats, Sophia carried a pitcher of tea over to their little table. "Jack, if you'd rather have a bottle of beer I'd be glad to get it for you. Otherwise, the tea is sweet and fresh."

He glanced at the young cook. "The tea will be fine, Sophia. Thanks."

"Where's Jazelle?" Vanessa asked. "At lunch she's usually in here helping Tallulah with the kids."

"She took a tray up to Kat a few minutes ago. In fact, she should've already made it back here to the kitchen. I'm beginning to wonder if something is wrong."

"I imagine the two women got to talking and the time has gotten away from both of them," Vanessa suggested.

"You're probably right," Sophia replied and gestured to the plate of pizza slices sitting in the middle of the table. "Let me know if you want more."

The cook went on about her business, and as Jack began to help himself to the pizza, Vanessa looked questioningly over at him.

"Why would you think it might not be okay with me to have lunch with you?"

Jack shrugged, then leaned slightly toward her and said in a lowered voice, "I've been thinking about the things I said to you last night. And... I figured you were probably angry with me."

"Angry? For having common sense? Not hardly, Jack."

He'd not expected her to react so casually about the whole thing. Especially after the way she'd kissed him. If it had gone on a few more seconds, he had no doubt they would have wound up in her bedroom or his. Would she have regretted having sex with him? No. It wasn't safe for him to even ask himself that question, he thought.

"I'm glad you didn't feel insulted. Because I didn't mean… None of what I said was meant to degrade you."

Shaking her head ever so slightly, she said, "I was disappointed, Jack. That's all. But after I thought about it, I realized that even feeling disappointed was stupid of me. After all, you can't change the circumstances of where you live or why you're here. Just like I can't change mine."

She could never begin to guess how empty and frustrated he was feeling about the situation. Yet he wasn't about to tell her his real thoughts on the matter. It would only make things worse. Besides, once the DNA test results came back, he'd be leaving.

"You're right. We can't change a thing." Not without one of them making huge sacrifices for the other.

She placed a slice of pizza onto her plate and cut off the point with her fork. "Do you have any idea when you might get the test results?"

"In three or four days, maybe. I understand a quicker test is available, but it's not quite as detailed or accurate. Blake and I both decided we wanted the test to be completely thorough."

"Of course." She lifted her eyes to his face. "So do you plan on leaving after you get the results?"

Strange, he thought, only last night Jack had told her that he missed his home in Utah. Yet even though he'd been speaking the truth, a part of him cringed at the idea of driving away and accepting the reality of never seeing Vanessa again.

"Jack? Did you hear me?"

Giving himself a hard, mental shake, he said, "Yeah. I heard you. I was just thinking about... things. But to answer your question, I suppose it will depend on the results. And, also, what you might come up with between now and then."

"Oh. Well, I should tell you I've been working all morning on a new site, and I did find your father's two brothers. But it still won't take me to the prior generation of Hollisters. I mean, it gives me a whopping list of people with the same name. However, none of them that I've gone through so far appears to fit with your family."

"What about Peter?"

She shook her head. "Nothing about him. I mean, yes, I've run across Peter Hollisters, but none that are the correct age. I might try different spellings or a name derived from Peter."

"That might make a difference." Resting his shoulders against the tall back of the wooden seat, he regarded her thoughtfully for a moment. "I've been thinking I need to do something for you, to show my appreciation for all the hard work you've been doing."

She let out a short laugh. "Not at all. Maureen is paying me for this—even though I offered to do the job for nothing. But she insists, and you can't argue with Maureen."

"You can't argue with me, either. Not about this,"

he told her, then smiled. "How about I take you out to dinner tomorrow night?"

Her eyes widened, and Jack could see the invitation had caught her off guard.

"Dinner? Where?"

He chuckled. "Since I don't know where anything is around here, you'll have to decide the place and the food. Anywhere you'd like to go is fine with me. As long as I don't have to wear a suit and tie. I didn't bring one with me."

Her eyes narrowed skeptically, and then she directed an impish smile at him. "Do you actually own a suit and tie?"

He laughed again. "Only one. It's mainly for funerals. And, thank God, I've not had to use it in a long time."

Her smile deepened. "Well, don't worry. I wouldn't choose that fancy a place, anyway."

"Does that mean you'll go?"

"I'd love to," she said. "Thank you for asking."

"My pleasure, Vanessa. I—"

His words suddenly broke off as he spotted Jazelle entering the kitchen and striding rapidly over to Tallulah. When she leaned down and whispered something in the nanny's ear, Jack decided something was amiss.

Frowning, Vanessa asked, "What's wrong? What are you looking at?"

"I think—"

Before he could finish, Jazelle approached their

table and motioned for Sophia, who was busy chopping vegetables at the cabinet counter, to join them.

"What's wrong?" Sophia asked the housekeeper.

"Nothing is wrong, exactly," Jazelle answered. "When Blake showed up a few minutes ago, Kat took one look at her husband and immediately grabbed her back. One pain is following another, so Blake is taking her to the hospital."

Her face wreathed in smiles, Vanessa clapped her hands together. "This is wonderful news!"

"Yippee! Finally! I can't wait to see them." Sophia let out a happy squeal and, grabbing Jazelle's hand, began to dance the housekeeper around in a tight circle.

Seeing the small commotion, Reeva left her spot at the stove to join them. "What's the celebrating about?"

Laughing, Sophia dropped her hold on Jazelle and turned to drop a kiss on her grandmother's cheek. "The babies are coming! Kat's having labor pains, and Blake is driving her to the hospital."

"It's about damned time," she muttered.

Feeling like an outsider, Jack glanced at the excited women grouped around him. "Is there anything I can do? I'll be glad to lend a hand if Blake needs me."

"Nice of you to offer, Jack. But Tag will make sure the hands take care of everything," Reeva told him.

Jack nodded that he understood, and Reeva went

back to her task at the stove. Sophia and Jazelle wandered back over to the table, where Tallulah was trying to calm the children's excitement at hearing the twins would soon be arriving.

Across the table, Vanessa let out a wistful sigh. "Two little babies. Can you imagine, Jack? Two to go with the three they already have. Kat and Blake are so blessed."

The stars he saw in Vanessa's eyes told him exactly how much she wanted a family of her own. The fact should've left him uneasy, and if she lived within normal driving distance of Stone Creek Ranch, it would have made him damned nervous. If Vanessa wanted two or eight kids, it was nothing to him. Some other man would be giving them to her.

"I think they both realize how fortunate they are," Jack said.

She watched him bite off a piece of pizza.

"You're probably thinking five children are a bit much," she said.

"Not for Blake. He has a knack for being a dad."

Her blue eyes made a slow survey of his face. "What about you? Five too many for you?"

Her question made him want to squirm, but fortunately he managed to curb the urge and gave her a cool little smile. "I won't ever be a dad, Vanessa. Not even to one child."

She frowned as though she wasn't quite certain

she'd heard him correctly. "No children? Why? You don't like them?"

"Sure. I like them." But to have a child with a woman, he'd have to trust her completely. And since he'd been fooled by Desiree, he hadn't run across any that he felt he could safely hand his heart to. "But it takes two to have children. And I'm a single guy."

"Hmm. And that's the way you want to stay— single," she said thoughtfully. "Well, everyone has their own ideas about what makes them happy. And following the tradition of growing into an adult, getting married and raising a family is what some people want, while others had rather take their life in a different direction. It's all about what wishes and wants we have in here."

Jack watched her tap a finger against the middle of her chest, and it was all he could do not to grimace and tell her that following her heart wasn't nearly as smart as letting her brain direct her through life.

"Some people follow this." He tapped a finger against his temple.

A twisted smile appeared on her lips. "I suppose that is the safe road to follow. But I'm not so sure it makes for a happy trail, Jack."

Jack wasn't sure, either. Not about these strong feelings of attraction he was developing toward Vanessa. As for being happy, he wasn't sure he'd ever experience true joy again. A heart needed to be free to feel happiness, and his wasn't. It was bound up with doubts and mistrust. And no matter how hard he tried to rid himself of the bitter past, he kept remembering it as a lesson learned.

Chapter Six

The next evening, as Jack fastened the pearl snaps on his western shirt, he leaned closer to the dresser mirror and peered at his face.

Damn! Even after shaving, he looked like he'd been on a three-day drunk. Fatigue had left dark crescents beneath his eyes and cut grooves from the corners of his mouth down to either side of his chin.

That's what he got for staying up most of the night, waiting to hear word about Blake and Katherine's new twins and then today, because Tag's crew had been shorthanded, he'd pitched in to help the foreman and ranch hands vaccinate cattle all day.

Well, missing the sleep was worth it, Jack thought, as he smoothed a brush through his wavy hair. Vanessa, Tallulah and Jim, and Reeva and Sophia had all remained in the den, anxiously waiting to hear from family members who'd gone to the hospital to wait with Blake.

When they'd finally received word around midnight that healthy twin boys had arrived and Katherine was comfortably recuperating, everyone had been incredibly happy. Including Vanessa, who'd grabbed Jack and smacked joyous kisses on both his cheeks.

Just seeing her so thrilled about the babies' arrival had lifted his spirits. How could he not feel joy when she and Sophia had danced around the den like carefree children? Yet at the same time, he'd felt a spurt of unexplainable loneliness. He felt as though he was watching a celebration that would always be for someone else and never him.

Hell, he was losing all common sense, he thought. Back at Stone Creek, he never went around thinking about things he was missing. Certainly not about having a wife or babies of his own. He didn't want or need those things. Being here on Three Rivers and seeing all these husbands and wives and babies was giving him a distorted view of love and marriage. These Hollisters lived in a fairy-tale world, while regular folks had to be content with grabbing a bit of pleasure here and there.

Like he intended to do tonight with Vanessa. Spending a few hours with her over dinner had to be enough for him. Wanting or expecting anything more would be inviting trouble and heartache.

Turning away from the dresser, Jack levered his hat onto his head, pulled on a jean jacket and walked down the hall to Vanessa's door.

She answered after his first knock, and Jack was momentarily caught off guard by her appearance. A black dress skimmed her luscious curves and red, high-heeled sandals boosted her height. Her long black hair was draped to one side and pinned away from her face with a rhinestone clip. He'd expected her to look lovely, but tonight she'd gone beyond that. Everything about her appearance was alluring and sexy, and he suddenly realized he was going to have hell sticking to his no-kissing plan.

"Mmm! You look beautiful," he told her.

The dazzling smile she shot back at him drew his attention straight to her red lips.

"Thank you, Jack. I made an extra effort tonight."

For him? Or because they were going to town and would be among other people? He wasn't going to ask.

"I'm a little early," he said. "If you need more time, I'll wait for you in the den."

"No need for that. Just let me get my things, and we'll go down together."

Leaving the door open, she disappeared into another part of the room. Seconds later she returned, carrying a red handbag and a black lacy wrap.

"All set," she said. "I hope you're hungry, because

I'm starving. And I don't want to eat like a pig unless you do."

"In that case, I'll be sure and make a hog of myself, too."

Chuckling at his reply, she shut the door behind her and then, as they started across the balcony, latched her arm around his.

Jack had never been a touchy-feely-type guy. Unless he was totally alone with a woman, he kept his hands to himself. But from the moment he'd met Vanessa, she'd not shown any hesitation about linking her arm to his or taking hold of his hand. Even then, he'd understood it was just her way and shouldn't be taken personally. Still, the contact had jolted him. Yet now that days had passed and he'd spent more time with her, he was beginning to expect her to reach for him. He even looked forward to it.

They descended the stairs and were making their way through the hall when Maureen's voice drifted from the open doorway leading into the den.

"I think Jack and Vanessa were going into town tonight for dinner," she was saying. "I'll ring his cell. Maybe they haven't left yet."

Jack paused, and Vanessa stopped to look at him with raised brows.

"Sounds like we better check with Maureen before we leave," she suggested.

"Right."

The two of them entered the den to see Blake and his brother Joseph, who was still wearing his deputy's uniform, standing in the middle of the room. Over by a wall table, Maureen was picking up a cell phone.

"Did I hear my name mentioned?" Jack asked.

At the sound of his voice, Maureen placed the phone back on the table and hurried over to him and Vanessa. Blake and Joseph followed directly behind their mother.

"Oh, Jack, I'm so glad you hadn't left yet," Maureen said. "We have news that you and Vanessa should hear."

Jack's gaze settled on Joseph. Since he'd been staying on the ranch, he'd only seen the young deputy a couple of times. Which, most likely, meant that the man hadn't driven over just to say hello and have a cocktail. "Has something bad happened?" He glanced anxiously at Blake. "Are the babies okay?"

The broad smile on Blake's face answered the question before he even spoke. "Randall and Russell are doing great. In fact, the boys and their mother are coming home tomorrow."

Jack was relieved. "That's good news."

Vanessa said to Blake, "I know you'll want to keep the babies away from everyone for a while so they won't be exposed to unwanted germs. So my only request is for you to take plenty of pics to show us."

Joseph chuckled. "Are you kidding? My brother's phone will probably quit working it'll be so jammed with pics," he said, and then his expression sobered. "Actually, Jack, the results of the DNA came into the sheriff's office no more than an hour ago. I came here to the ranch to give you all the news in person."

Jack was totally surprised. "They're already back? We were told it would take three or four days!"

Joseph said, "Guess the lab wasn't backlogged."

Jack could feel Vanessa dart an anxious look at him; meanwhile, Maureen made a hurry-up motion at Joseph.

"Okay, Joe," she said impatiently. "Both men are here, and I'm here. So out with it. What did the test show?"

Joe somberly looked at the four of them, then suddenly grinned. "Okay. Hold on to your reins. It says Jack is our relative. A ninety-nine-and-something-percent conclusive chance. I'll have to dig out the paper to show you."

While Joe reached inside his jeans pocket, Jack stared in shocked wonder at Blake and Maureen.

"I-is this for real?" he asked in a dazed voice.

Blake stepped forward and placed a hand on Jack's shoulder. "I not only have two new sons, I have another new relative, too. Welcome to the family, Jack. Whatever you are—nephew, uncle, cousin—I'm happy about this." He glanced at Maureen. "How do you feel about it, Mom?"

Tears glistened in her eyes. "I felt it all along. That first day Jack arrived, I'm sure he thought I was crazy. I kept going on about him having Chandler's eyes. But I was right and now…" She turned to Jack and gave him a tight hug. "Distant or close, you're family, Jack. I'm thrilled, and I'm certain Gil will be, too."

As Maureen stepped back, Jack was dismayed at the lump of emotion lodged in his throat. After a hard swallow, he finally managed to speak. "I don't know what to say."

Joseph chuckled. "I can understand you being a little rattled. We're kind of a rowdy bunch. You might not want to be related to us."

"I'd better warn you, Joe, my bunch is rowdy, too." Jack tried to laugh, but the attempt choked him, and he swiped a hand over his face in an effort to compose himself. "This...doesn't seem real."

Joseph handed the paper with the test results to his mother. "I guess we should all know better than to question your instincts, Mom."

She read the written information and, with a smug smile on her face, passed it to Jack.

"So what now, Maureen?" Vanessa asked. "Where do we go from here?"

"I'm not sure. We now know for certain that the two families are related. But we don't have a clue as to how or where we're connected." She leveled a questioning look at Vanessa. "Are you willing to keep on with this search?"

"Of course. Even if it takes months, I have until the end of December. After that, I can do the genealogy search on weekends," she said.

So everything was coming to a close, Jack thought. At least, the first step of this mystery had reached an end. Which meant he'd be leaving Three Rivers Ranch soon. The idea saddened him as much as learning he was a relative of this family had surprised him.

Frowning, Blake asked Vanessa, "You think finding the answers might take a long time?"

She said, "From the walls I've run into so far, I do. But I'm positive we'll figure everything out—eventually."

Still feeling a bit dazed, Jack reached out and shook both Blake's and Joseph's hands before he turned to Maureen and placed a gentle kiss on her cheek.

"Thank you, Maureen. If not for you, none of us would've known about any of this. And that would've been a great loss for me. All of you have been...well, the best."

"Just wait until you really get to know us," Maureen teased, and then suddenly blinked at the moisture in her eyes. "Sorry, everyone. I didn't mean to get emotional This is a happy occasion. I keep thinking about Joel and wishing he could've known about this."

Joseph stepped forward and curled an arm around his mother's shoulders. "I'm thinking Dad does know about it, Mom. He's probably looking down on us right now and smiling."

"I'm not so sure," Jack attempted to joke. "He might be seeing my family and groaning."

Blake shook his head. "If they're all like you, Jack, we know Dad would be proud."

The mention of the late Mr. Hollister caused Jack to suddenly think of his own father. "It just dawned on me that my family needs to hear the news. I should call Dad and let him know. He can tell the others." He turned a regretful look at Vanessa. "I hate asking, but would you mind being a bit late to dinner?"

Before Vanessa could say a word, Maureen interjected, "There's no need for you to delay your dinner plans, Jack. I'll be happy to call your father and give him the news. Since I'm the one who first called him about all this, it's only fitting that he hears the results from me. You two go on and enjoy the evening."

"Mom is right, Jack," Blake said. "You'll have plenty of time to talk this over with your dad later."

After a few more words of encouragement, Jack decided they were right, and he and Vanessa left the house and walked out to his truck.

Along the way, Vanessa said, "Really, Jack, if you're thinking you need to have a long talk with your father, don't let me stop you. We can always stay here and eat Reeva and Sophia's cooking."

"As good as their meals are, I'm looking forward to this night out, Vanessa. And like Maureen said, she can tell Dad everything I could tell him. I'll call him early in the morning. That will give him time to sleep on the news."

"What do you think he's going to say about it?"

Jack chuckled. "I've never known Dad to be

speechless, but he just might be when he gets this news."

After helping her into the truck, he took his place in the driver's seat and started the engine but stopped short of putting the truck into gear. Instead, he looked over at her.

"So what do you think about this revelation, Vanessa? And don't soft-soap it. Tell me what you really think."

Shrugging, she said, "I can't speak for the rest of your family, but as for you, I think it's going to be a good thing. Even before the test results came in, I got the feeling that you were already thinking of these Hollisters as your family. The DNA just made it official."

"Yeah. I think you're right."

Still thoughtful, he put the truck into gear and drove away from the house.

By the time they reached the town of Wickenburg, they had decided to eat at Jose's Restaurant, which was located on the southwestern edge of town where the desert terrain stretched for empty miles. The building was a sprawling hacienda style with stucco walls painted pale turquoise. Graceful arches supported a red-tiled roof that hung over a ground-level porch, which ran the entire width of the structure. Each arch was decorated with strings of colorful gourds and bright red peppers. At one end of the porch, a bougainvillea covered with yellow-gold blossoms climbed to the top of the porch roof, while a fat saguaro with two sturdy arms stood at the opposite end.

The graveled parking lot was filled with vehicles, and as the two of them made their way to the entrance, Jack said, "Looks like a popular eating place. Do you come here often?"

"The food is fabulous so it's very popular. Not to mention the view out here is spectacular. But I don't come here on a frequent basis. Usually just for special occasions. Like a friend's birthday or whenever my parents come up from Phoenix."

"I see. You don't want to turn a special thing into something mundane. Right?"

Surprised that he understood, she flashed him a brief smile. "Exactly. Too much of a good thing can be bad for a person."

He smiled back at her. "You say that like you have vices."

Only regarding a sexy Utah rancher, she thought glumly. But even her feelings for Jack were soon going to come to an end.

"From time to time, we all have a few, don't we?"

He chuckled under his breath. "I'll confess to a few."

With his hand resting gently against the small of her back, the two of them entered the restaurant and were promptly met by a hostess. The young woman with long brown hair and a red floor-length skirt collected menus from a wooden podium and guided them back to a corner table located near a tall, arched window.

After they were seated at the small round table and a waitress had taken orders for their drinks, Jack glanced toward the window and a view of the desert.

"The Joshua trees and saguaros sure are pretty," he said reflectively. "This sort of looks like the land west of the Three Rivers Ranch house. Where you showed me the North Star. Remember?"

Remember? Those moments had been burned into her memory. Even if she never saw him again for the rest of her life, she'd always have those special moments to relive in her mind.

The thought unexpectedly caused her throat to tighten, and she wished the waitress would get back with their drinks. She didn't want Jack to think she was getting emotional. Especially because she could feel their time together winding to a close.

"I do. And I just happen to know a place not too far west of here where there's another special view of the evening star."

His eyelids lowered ever so slightly as he looked across the table at her. "After we eat you should show me."

Did he expect her to look at him in the moonlight and not feel the urge to kiss him? Or maybe she'd get lucky, Vanessa thought, and the moon would be in a new phase and the light would be too weak to illuminate his face.

Damn it, Vanessa. Who are you fooling? You could find Jack's lips in the darkest of nights.

Thankfully, a waitress suddenly approached their table, and the distraction pushed the mocking voice from her head. But not the idea of being in Jack's arms again. She was beginning to fear she'd never rid herself of that longing.

For the next few minutes, while waiting for their meal to be served, they munched on tortilla chips and salsa and sipped frozen margaritas. The food and drink eased the emptiness of her stomach, but as time ticked on, Vanessa found herself doing most of the talking and Jack giving her one-word responses.

She could understand why he was preoccupied. No doubt he was still stunned to have learned he was related to one of the wealthiest and most prestigious families in Arizona. But understanding didn't wipe away her disappointment. From the moment Jack had asked Vanessa to go out with him for dinner, she'd been looking forward to spending this time with him, away from the distractions of the ranch. Yet the arrival of the DNA results had ruined any chance of her holding his attention.

"I feel guilty about us being out tonight," Vanessa said to him as she plucked another tortilla chip from the basket. "You probably should have stayed at the ranch and called your father. And talked all of this out with the Hollister brothers."

He scowled at her. "Why do you say that?"

She chewed her chip and washed it down with a

sip of the icy drink. "These past few minutes you've gone off to another world. Are you concerned about your family's reaction to this news?"

"No. If any of them has reservations, they'll just have to get over them. That's the way I feel about it. After all, it's a certainty you can't change bloodlines." His expression turned rueful as he met her gaze. "I'm sorry if I've seemed distracted. I've been thinking."

"Obviously."

A faint smile touched his lips, and Vanessa wished she could focus on something other than his face. He'd probably already noticed she'd been staring at him, but she couldn't seem to help herself. She couldn't pinpoint the reason he looked even more handsome than usual tonight. Perhaps the difference had something to do with the tan shirt stretched across his broad shoulders or the way his dark brown hair glistened in the glow of the flickering candlelight. Or was she mesmerized with his appearance because she'd already become infatuated with the guy?

"Yes, obviously," he replied. "And I have to admit I've surprised myself."

"How have you managed to do that?"

His gaze moved to the view beyond the window. "Now that the test results are back, I'll be leaving for Utah soon. And I'm not sure how I feel about that."

Vanessa didn't have to ask herself how she felt about the reality of the situation. The thought of him leaving made her sad. And yet, she continued to tell herself their parting would be for the best. He'd already told her he wasn't a family man. Even if he stayed here for another month or two or three, he'd still be that same man who wanted to remain free and single. And she'd be crazy to believe she could change him.

"What do you mean?" she asked. "Aren't you excited about getting back to your home, to Stone Creek Ranch?"

"I do miss my ranch." He shrugged and picked up his margarita. "But that doesn't mean I won't miss Three Rivers and everyone there. I'm sure going to miss you, Vanessa."

Her heart made a weird leap, then took off at a gallop. Was this the same guy who'd suggested they shouldn't kiss or get close? Didn't he know he was sending her all sorts of mixed signals?

When she spoke her voice was hoarse. "Right now you believe you'll miss me, but once you get home, I'll just be a speck in your memory."

His vivid blue gaze moved away from the window to connect with hers. "You think so?"

His voice was soft and skittered over her skin like a warm caress. She wrapped her fingers around the glass containing the frozen drink and hoped the icy temperature would cool the stinging heat in her cheeks. "I do honestly believe that."

"So should I assume that once I leave, you're going to forget all about me?" he asked.

Forget him? About as likely as she'd forget the first night they'd met and she'd taken him out to the rock climb. A hundred years wouldn't erase him from her mind. But confessing that much to him would only create complications for both of them.

"I'm going to be researching your family," she said in the most casual voice she could muster. "I can hardly look at your name every day and forget you."

"Hmm. I wasn't thinking of the research. If you're lucky you'll soon find the clue you need, and then the missing tree branch will appear."

When Vanessa had first accepted Maureen's request to help her with her family ancestry, she'd been excited to dig into the job. History was her subject, and exploring the Hollisters was something she'd been eager to do. Never in her wildest dreams had she thought the task would lead her to Jack or these strong feelings she was beginning to feel for him.

"Maybe," she murmured.

"Let's not talk about the relative thing anymore. Tell me what your life is like when school is in session and you're teaching."

Groaning, she smiled at him. "I'm not sure we have that much time, Jack."

He chuckled. "Sure, we do. We have all night."

Vanessa's company, along with the good food and tequila, helped to ease the initial shock he'd felt upon hearing the DNA results. And by the time the two of them left Jose's he was thinking clearly. At least as far the reality of being related to the Three River Hollisters. As for Vanessa, his mind was a jumbled mess, and what was worse, he feared she knew it.

He should never have told her that he was going to miss her. That had been stupid of him, and he figured the tequila he'd consumed had been partially to blame for the admission. But hell, why try to avoid the truth? He was going to miss her. Even if he never kissed her or held her in his arms again, he would still miss seeing her beautiful face and hearing her sweet voice and happy laugh. And the way she reached for his hand or arm… Oh yes, he was going to miss that, too.

"Jack, we don't have to take a stargazing drive unless you want to. It's still early. You could drive home to the ranch and talk with the Hollisters."

He frowned as he gently cupped a hand beneath her elbow and helped her into the truck. "Will you quit with the Hollisters? This time is yours and ours. Let's enjoy it. Okay?"

She smiled at him. "Okay. No more about the Hollisters. For the next few minutes you're going to get a science lesson in astronomy."

Chuckling, he made an exaggerated wipe of his forehead. "Whew! For a minute there, I was afraid you were going to say *history.*"

"Jack!"

Laughing, he closed the passenger door of the truck, then promptly joined her on his side of the cab.

"I was only teasing. You can give me a history

lesson if you like. Dad always says a man is never too old to learn."

He drove the truck out of the parking lot and turned westward onto a highway leading into the desert.

"Sounds like your father is a smart man," she said with a smug smile. "But actually, you might like hearing about the gold rush that happened around here back in the 1800s. In fact, some gold is still being found."

"I overheard Maureen talking about the Gold Rush Days celebration that occurs annually here in town. From what she said, the festival started because of the big mines that were discovered near Wickenburg."

"Oh, shoot. So you already know about that. Well, I'll bet you didn't know that Chandler's assistant Trey and his wife, Nicole, like to pan for nuggets. And they've found several small chunks of gold recently. They're saving them up to buy a ranch."

"That's interesting. Did they find the gold close by?"

"Not exactly. But the location is in Yavapai County. I know it's dark, but can you see that mountain to the north?" She pointed her finger toward a ridge of mountains visible through her side window.

"Barely. But I do."

"Well, you go to the mountain beyond that one, and there's a canyon there on land that belongs to a friend of Trey's. There's a stream at the bottom of the canyon, and that's where they pan. Nicole says that even in the driest part of the summer there's usually water there. So I'm thinking it must be spring-fed."

"Hmm. We've been told that gold was once discovered on our property. Long before it became Stone Creek Ranch. And Hunter and I did find pieces of an old wooden trellis used for washing ore down by the river. But we've never bothered to look for any nuggets or placer. I think that's what the gold particles in the sand and gravel are called."

She looked at him. "Why? You're not interested in that sort of thing?"

"I never really thought much about it," he told her. "For one thing, it's doubtful that anyone ever got rich off the placer—I mean, not by finding minerals. If they did, we never heard about it. And Dad always laughed at the idea. He sees dollars in cattle and sheep."

"Well, everyone has a different definition of a treasure. My mother thinks it's propping up her feet and drinking a cup of coffee."

Jack grunted with amusement. "She sounds like a woman who's easy to please."

"She is. That's why Dad calls her his treasure."

"Your parents must love each other," he said.

She darted a confused look at him. "Of course they do. Don't yours?" she asked and then immediately shook her head. "Forgive me, Jack. That didn't come out right. I'm sure your parents are crazy about each other. After eight children and all these years, they'd have to be."

"Yeah, they'd have to be," he said flatly. "But they're not like Maureen and Gil."

She let out a soft laugh. "What couple is like Maureen and Gil? They're… Well, their relationship is mystical or something. I can't describe it. And anyway, every couple is different. Every love is different."

Vanessa was right about that, he thought somewhat cynically. It either lasted or it didn't. And Jack's hadn't lasted. At least that had been his thinking after his breakup with Desiree. But in these past few days, since he'd met Vanessa, he'd been looking back on his relationship with Desiree and wondering why he'd ever thought he'd loved her, much less wanted to marry her. Nothing he'd felt for her had been close to the real thing.

"Different," he repeated. "That's one way of putting it."

She didn't make any comment, and Jack kept his focus on the lonely strip of highway stretching in front of him.

After a couple of minutes passed, she said, "Stop at this pull-off, Jack. This is the spot I wanted you to see."

He slowed the truck and steered it onto a small graveled area. As he brought it to a stop, he glanced over at her. "We just passed a huge turnout on the hill behind us. Why not stop there instead?"

Her grin was indulgent. "Because the view from here is better. Never leave stargazing up to highway engineers, Jack."

He chuckled. "Is that part of tonight's lesson in astronomy?"

Her grin turned into a smile, and Jack thought how nice it was that he could tease her and know she wouldn't be offended. With most of the women he'd dated in the past, he'd had to watch his words carefully. With Vanessa he could be himself.

"Yes, let that be lesson number one."

He shut off the motor and slanted her a sly look. "Okay, teacher, how did you come about finding this spot on the road for stargazing? Driving around with an old flame?"

"I expected you to think as much. But no, I actually found it by accident. I had made a trip over to California to visit a girlfriend in Big Bear. On my way back my car started making a strange noise so I pulled over." She unsnapped her seat belt and reached for the door latch. "Come on. Let's look."

Once they were outside the truck, Vanessa reached for his hand, and Jack allowed her to lead him across the small parking area and onto a dim trail.

"Aren't you a bit worried about sidewinders out here?" he asked dubiously, then chuckled. "Pardon the question. I forgot about your ability to see like a cat."

"Well, maybe not as accurately as a cat, but I think I'd see a sidewinder."

They passed several boulders and a stand of yucca trees before they reached the top of an incline and Vanessa finally came to a halt.

"Okay," he said skeptically, "most people don't go off hiking whenever they're having car trouble. How did you end up here?"

Her light laugh said she enjoyed confusing him. "I didn't hike out here that night," she corrected him. "I got out of my car to let it sit quiet for a few minutes and just happened to look up and notice the panoramic view of the sky. So a few days later I drove back out here and did a little exploring. I don't come out here often, but I like to come around Christmastime. Sort of makes me feel like a wise man or shepherd."

He glanced down at her glowing face, and Jack thought how her eyes outshone any star in the sky.

"Now you're probably thinking I'm the corniest woman you've ever met," she said softly.

No, Jack thought, he was thinking her heart was far too soft for a man like him. The bitter gall he carried around inside him seemed to be stuck there permanently. But when he looked at Vanessa, especially like this, with a bit of moonlight bathing her face with silver light, he wished he could rid himself of all the bottled-up humiliation and resentment.

"Not at all, Vanessa," he said softly. "I think you're...pretty special."

Her lashes fluttered, and the tip of her tongue ran

over her lips. "Jack, you're supposed to be looking at the stars. Not at me."

"True. But my eyes would rather be on you."

Her nostrils flared as she drew in a sharp breath. "Why are you saying something like this when... you don't want us to kiss? Or have you forgotten?"

"I've not forgotten. And you're wrong. I do want us to kiss, but I believe we...shouldn't." As if they had a will of their own, his hands came to rest on the tops of her shoulders, and his eyes focused on her lips. "Because when I put my lips on yours...well, one kiss leads to another. And another. I'm afraid that once I start I might not be able to stop."

She turned just enough to align the front of her body with his. "Have you ever thought that I might not want you to stop?"

A rush of indescribable emotions caused his throat to tighten and turn his voice raspy. "I've thought of that too many times. And right now, I don't want to think. I just want to feel you in my arms."

She whispered his name, and then suddenly her arms were around his neck, and her lips connected with his.

To finally be kissing her again was like coming home after a long, long journey. Familiar, sweet, in-credible. The sensations swirled inside him until his brain ceased to think and his body took over.

Even if he'd had enough sense to stop himself from pulling her into his arms and devouring her lips with his, he wouldn't have found the strength to set her apart from him. Being connected to Vanessa was everything he wanted. Just kissing her filled him with a pleasure that knew no bounds and made him wonder what making love to her would do to his psyche. He doubted he'd ever recover. A night in her bed would only make him want more and more. Just as he was wanting her now.

Seconds ticked by, and as the kiss deepened, he drew her tight in the circle of his arms until her breasts were pressed flat against his chest. Instinctively, their tongues met and began a slow tango that shot hot desire straight to Jack's loins. And with a needy groan, his hands dropped to her buttocks and gripped her hips tight against the throbbing bulge behind the fly of his jeans.

Somewhere above the roaring in his ears, he heard her soft moans. The sound mingled with the soft desert breeze and acted on his senses like accelerant to a fire that was already out of control.

Eventually, the need for oxygen and the distant flash of headlights from a passing vehicle were enough to give Jack the strength to lift his head and put an end to the fiery embrace.

"Jack," she whispered in a dazed voice, "am I still standing upright?"

"Yes. But only because I'm holding you."

"Oh."

She let out a heavy breath, and then to his dismay, she rested her cheek against the middle of his chest.

"I'm so glad you are holding me," she told him.

Closing his eyes, his hand came up and stroked the back of her long hair. "You were right a few minutes ago. When we're together we go offtrack. And—"

The remainder of his sentence halted as she lifted her head to look at him. "Please, don't ruin this moment with a lecture. We kissed, okay? It got passionate, okay? We're a man and a woman with combustive chemistry. I'd be happy if you'd leave it at that."

The beseeching expression on her face made him want to give her whatever she wanted, even though he wasn't capable. Especially if her wants involved his heart.

He let out a heavy breath. "All right, no lectures. But we should probably head back. It's a long drive from here to Three Rivers."

Especially when he was going to have to fight every mile of the way to keep from stopping the truck and pulling her into his arms.

Chapter Seven

Vanessa groaned with frustration as she scanned the information on the monitor screen. Peter A. Hollister. She'd found several persons with the same name, but none with an age that would fit Hadley's grandfather. She needed to find a man with a birthday dating back a hundred years or more. So far she couldn't even come up with where or when his grandfather had been born.

Sighing, she leaned back in the executive chair and closed her eyes. Two days had passed since the night they'd had dinner at Jose's, and during that time she'd seen very little of Jack. And when she had, there had been a group of people around.

Clearly, he'd been purposely avoiding being alone

with her. But it was pointless to let that fact get to her now. During dinner last night, he'd announced he'd be leaving for Utah in the morning. And telling him goodbye wasn't going to be easy.

"Knock, knock!"

Vanessa opened her eyes to see Maureen stepping into the study. From the looks of her dusty clothes and cowboy hat, she'd been busy.

"Hi, Maureen. Looks like you've been working hard."

She eased into one of the chairs facing the desk and lifting her hat from her head, ran a hand over her shoulder-length hair. "Not really. Gil and I have been scouring the arroyos for calves. It's a fun job."

Their relationship is mystical.

The night she and Jack had had dinner out and the subject of love had entered the conversation, she'd noticed a sardonic tone creeping into Jack's voice. He'd implied his parents had gone through a shaky period of their marriage, but she didn't believe that was the reason for his jaded outlook on marriage. No, she got the feeling a woman had broken his heart and left him full of bitterness. And that notion bothered her far more than she cared to admit.

Vanessa smiled shrewdly. "You must have finished early or you came in to see the twins."

Katherine and the infant boys had arrived home yesterday and since then there had been a slew of well-wishers stopping by the ranch to leave gifts for the new babies. However, the only people who'd been allowed upstairs to actually visit the newborns were Gil and Maureen and Tallulah.

"As soon as I change out of these dirty clothes, I'm going upstairs," she said. "Katherine and Tallulah need a little break. And I need some time with my new grandsons."

Vanessa's smile was wistful. "The pics Blake has been showing everyone are adorable. He's obviously walking on air."

Maureen laughed. "That's an understatement! And everyone is telling him how the boys are the spitting image of him."

How would it feel, Vanessa wondered, to have a son who looked like Jack? How would it feel to be loved by him? To make a family with him?

Shaking the foolish questions from her mind, she said, "Yes, from the photos I've seen, I'd say they look like their daddy."

"Well, the reason I stopped by the study was to see if you've found anything on Peter Hollister today? Or Lionel?"

Vanessa rubbed fingers against the furrows in her brow. "Honestly, Maureen, I'm beginning to think I need to call my old history professor down at Phoenix. He's an expert on genealogy. He might give me some ideas on how to move forward."

Maureen grimaced. "In other words, no luck?"

"None. I keep striking out. Something just isn't jiving. Maybe when Jack gets—"

She stopped as a light knock sounded on the door.

"Come in," Maureen called.

Expecting to see Jazelle with a fresh pot of coffee, Vanessa was a bit surprised to see Jack entering the study.

"Excuse me. I didn't mean to interrupt," he said as he eyed the two women. "I'll come back later."

"No. You'll come in now," Maureen insisted. "In fact, you couldn't have picked a better time. Van was just about to say something about you."

He looked at Vanessa, and as their gazes met, she felt something in the middle of her chest tighten into an unbearable knot.

He said, "I hope it was something nice."

"Of course it would be nice." Maureen laughed lightly. "Van doesn't say mean things about anyone. She's too much of a lady."

Vanessa chuckled. "Boy, do I ever have you fooled, Maureen."

Smiling at that remark, Maureen turned her attention to Jack. "Was there something you needed to talk with Vanessa about in private?"

He walked over and eased into a chair that was angled toward Maureen's. "Actually, it's good that you're here, Maureen. I need to talk to you both—together."

Curious now, Vanessa's gaze switched between him and Maureen. "I hope you've come to tell us you've learned some pertinent information from your father. I'm stuck in the mud here."

He grimaced. "I just got off the phone with Dad.

He says he and Mom can't find any concrete birth documentation about Grandfather Lionel or his father, Peter."

Maureen frowned thoughtfully. "Jack, didn't I hear you say that your grandfather was buried somewhere on Stone Creek Ranch? Maybe the date of his birth is on a headstone or some other sort of marker."

"My brother Quint has already ridden out to the grave to look. The only thing written on the marker is *Lionel Hollister* and the date of his death. Dad seems to remember at the time they buried him that his birth certificate couldn't be located. But as best as he can recall, his father was born in December of 1941, but he's not a hundred percent certain."

"Surely you acknowledged his birthdays in some way while he was still living," Vanessa suggested.

"I imagine so," Jack replied. "But I was just a little kid when Lionel passed away. I don't remember all that much about him."

"Well, I wouldn't worry," Maureen told him. "I imagine he can write the state of Utah for a replica of his father's birth certificate. Was that all Hadley had to say on the matter?"

"No, he made a suggestion."

Jack glanced over to Vanessa, and there was something about the stark look on his face that left her uneasy. Had she done or said something pertaining to the ancestry search that had angered his father?

Before Vanessa could question him, he said,

"When I leave for Stone Creek tomorrow, Dad wants you to join me. He'd like you to continue the genealogy search up there. He says there are mounds of old papers up in the attic that might serve as clues to his past family. Things that he's not bothered to look at since his father died."

Stunned, Vanessa stared at him. "Are you serious? Hadley wants me to stay at Stone Creek?"

"I'm telling you exactly what Dad would like," he said bluntly. "But that doesn't mean you have to agree to making the trip."

Go to Utah? With Jack? Her first thought was that she wouldn't be telling him goodbye. At least, not tomorrow. But just as quickly her mind was boggled with uncertainties. Being near the man for an extended length of time would be dangerous. Not only to her peace of mind but also to the well-being of her heart.

"I'm stunned. I don't know what to say," she murmured.

"Well, I do," Maureen suddenly said. "Hadley is making good sense. All the stumbling blocks are pointing toward his father and grandfather. Where better to search than at Stone Creek?"

"What you're saying does sound logical, Maureen. But you're the one who hired me, and—"

Ignoring Vanessa's protest, Jack addressed Maureen. "Dad understands that Vanessa is your employee. But now that it's been confirmed that our two families are related, he feels responsible to help with the search expense. He's willing to pay Vanessa's wages while she's at Stone Creek."

With a shake of her head, Maureen rose to her feet. "Nonsense. This is my doing. I'll take care of Vanessa's pay. All you need to do is talk her into making the trip with you."

Feeling slightly panicked, Vanessa said, "Maureen, I'll need to think about this. There are—"

The woman gave her a backward wave as she headed to the door. "Jack will give you time to think about it, Van. Besides, you don't have a thing to worry about."

With that bit of advice, she left the room and Vanessa let out a pent-up breath. "Wow! I never saw this coming," she said quietly.

"Neither did I."

Her gaze slipped over his face, and for the first time since he'd entered the room, she noticed there were dried patches of sweat on his denim shirt, along with several coats of dust. His willingness to blend in with the family and ranch crew spoke volumes about his character, Vanessa thought. He clearly didn't shy away from work. But getting close to her was a whole other matter.

She said, "You don't sound the least bit happy about your father's suggestion."

"I didn't say anything about being unhappy."

"You didn't have to," she retorted. "I can see it on your face."

A scowl pulled his brows together. "I'm not upset, if that's what you're thinking. Just a little uneasy."

She left her seat and walked over to the window. With her back to him, she said, "I imagine you're worried I'll throw myself at you and generally make a pest of myself. If so, you can toss that concern out the window."

"What's that supposed to mean? You sound angry with me."

Closing her eyes, she pinched the bridge of her nose. She didn't know why she was saying such things to him. To salvage her pride, she supposed. Besides, telling him how she really felt was totally off the table.

"I'm not angry," she said. "More like…a bit hurt."

Suddenly he was standing behind her, and Vanessa's insides trembled as his hand came to rest on the back of her shoulder.

"How have I hurt you?"

The sincerity in his voice made her groan. "Other than made me feel unwanted, you haven't done anything."

"Unwanted? Are you joking?"

She felt like an idiot. She'd known from the very start that his stay here would be brief. Moreover, he'd made it clear he wanted to remain free and single. She should have kept a friendly distance between them. Instead, she'd practically begged him to make love to her.

"I'm not talking about wanting me physically.

I can see that you don't want me on Stone Creek Ranch. But that's okay. If I agree to go, it won't be for your sake. It'll be because your father wants me to go."

"You don't know what you're saying," he muttered.

She blinked her burning eyes, then bracing herself turned to face him. "Look, Jack, you could have said you thought your father's idea for me to go to Stone Creek was a good one. Instead, you're trying to think of every possible way to discourage me and not look like a jerk while you're doing it."

His fingers gently tightened on the ridge of her shoulder. "You have it all wrong, Vanessa."

"Do I?"

"Yes, you do. When Dad told me what he wanted I was… A part of me was thrilled that I wasn't going to have to say goodbye. And that we'd have a chance to have each other's company for a while longer. But—"

"Yes, the big *but* is that you don't want to have to deal with the temptation of having sex with me," she said bluntly.

A dark red blush crept up his throat and onto his face. "Okay. That much is true. I don't want us to get into a situation where you might get hurt."

Leveling a pointed look at him, she said, "Why don't you say what you're really thinking? That *you* don't want to get hurt."

The corners of his mouth curved downward. "You're right. I am thinking about myself, too."

"Well, you can rest easy, Jack. Since we had dinner at Jose's, I've done plenty of thinking, and I've come to the conclusion that I shouldn't have thrown myself at you that night. It won't happen again."

He groaned. "Oh, Vanessa, nothing remotely close to that ever crossed my mind. You weren't exactly twisting my arm." His eyes met hers. "But there's more to consider now. Dad and Maureen are counting on you to complete this Hollister puzzle. We can't let our feelings stand in the way of their wishes."

Her heart thudding heavily, she connected her gaze with his. "Are you trying to say you want me to go?"

He breathed deeply. "Yes. We're friends, aren't we? We can act like adults."

It might take loads of acting ability on her part, but she could make herself be cool and adult on the outside. She'd make sure that no one would suspect her of falling for Jack. Besides, she hadn't fallen for him, she mentally argued. She'd just had a momentary lapse of sanity.

"Yes. We're friends," she told him.

"So maybe you should start packing, and I'll call Dad and tell him to expect us home by tomorrow evening."

Home with Jack. Such a thing would never happen emotionally, Vanessa thought. But this trip could prove to be the next thing to it. And that meant she was headed straight for heartache.

* * *

The sun had barely risen over the eastern ridge of mountains when Jack drove slowly away from Three Rivers Ranch. And though he didn't look in the rearview mirror, he sensed the group of people standing on the wide steps of the porch were still there, waving goodbye.

He'd not expected such a feeling of melancholy to strike him over leaving the place. Hell, he'd only known these folks for a few days. They couldn't have grown to mean so much to him in such a short time, he thought. But the tightness in his throat proved otherwise.

Swallowing hard, he glanced across to the passenger seat, where Vanessa was giving one last wave out the window.

"Jazelle and Sophia were crying when they kissed you goodbye," he said to her. "They obviously hated to see you go. They're acting like you're going to be gone to Utah for months and months. At the most you can only stay until school starts the first of January. And who knows, you might solve the whole family tree thing in a week or two."

Sighing, she pushed the button to raise the window, then straightened around in her seat.

"Yes, I know. But Jazelle and I have been close friends for years. And Sophia has been my friend ever since she moved here in November of last year. I'm going to miss seeing them every day."

"No doubt," he replied.

She glanced at him. "I could say the same about Blake and Taggart. Both guys looked downright sad to see you go. I think you've made new friends. Not just with them but with everyone at Three Rivers."

"I'll be honest, Vanessa. Seeing this ranch and being with the family has been an eye-opener for me. I thought I'd be happy when this day finally arrived. Instead, I've already promised Maureen and Gil to make a return visit before too long."

"I'm glad it all turned out so well for you, Jack. Especially when you didn't know what you might be walking into."

He tried to smile as he focused on the narrow dirt road in front of them "I honestly expected the Hollisters to look down their noses at me. And I thought the ranch hands would be know-it-alls and brag about doing everything better."

Vanessa chuckled. "That's funny."

"Yeah. Very funny," he admitted, then glanced at her. He couldn't begin to guess what she was actually feeling about this trip ahead of them. He did know one thing, though. Ever since they'd talked in the study yesterday afternoon, she'd kept her distance from him.

Whether that was because she'd been busy packing for her stay at Stone Creek or because she was still irked with him, he didn't know. And he'd decided it was probably for the best if he let the subject drop. For the next several hours they were going to be cooped up together in the cab of the truck. He didn't want to add to the tension.

"Are you looking forward to this drive? Or would you rather be flying?"

Her smile was faint. "I actually like driving best. That way you can see everything on the way. I'm one of those people who thinks the travel is often the best part of a journey. I'm looking forward to seeing Stone Creek Ranch and meeting your family, too."

"I hope you're not disappointed," he said.

Smiling, she turned in the seat so that she was facing him. "I won't be. But I am concerned that I might let your father down. If I can't unravel this ancestry mystery, he's going to be unhappy."

"Dad doesn't expect miracles, Vanessa. All he ever asks from anyone is that they put out their best effort. And I already know you're going to do that."

"That's nice of you to say," she said quietly, then turned her attention on the landscape passing by the window.

Nice. Maybe that was Jack's whole problem, he thought, as he tried to ignore Vanessa's presence. Maybe if he'd not pulled away from Vanessa the other night and made love to her instead, things would be a whole heck of a lot better between them now. After all, women were different nowadays. Going to bed with a man didn't necessarily mean she wanted to marry him.

Don't be stupid, Jack. Vanessa isn't a woman who has a casual view of sex. She's the loving, marry-

ing kind. And no matter how long she stays at Stone Creek or how close she gets, you have to remember that.

The mocking voice in Jack's head irritated him to no end. He shoved it away, and for the next twenty minutes focused on the long, rough drive that would take them off Three Rivers Ranch and ultimately onto the main highway.

When they reached the town of Kingman some three hours later, Jack stopped at a gas station to fill up, and Vanessa used the opportunity to visit the restroom before they climbed back into the truck and headed north. It wasn't until they'd crossed over into Utah and entered the outskirts of St. George that Jack suggested they stop to stretch their legs and eat.

At a popular chain restaurant, they carried meals of burgers and fries to an outdoor patio furnished with tables shaded by huge umbrellas.

The weather was just shy of being hot, while a brisk wind blew Vanessa's hair in every direction. As soon as they were seated, she pulled a scrunchie from her purse.

As she used the red piece of fabric to twist her hair into a ponytail, she said, "This will save me from eating hair with my burger."

"It is windy out here. You might be more comfortable if we go back inside," he suggested.

"Thanks for the offer, but I'm fine." She took a sip

of cola and unwrapped her sandwich. "How much farther to Stone Creek?"

"Two hours or a little more. Are you getting tired?"

She shook her head. "A bit stiff from sitting, that's all."

He opened his burger and sprinkled the contents with an ample amount of salt and pepper. The simple task drew Vanessa's eyes to his hands, and she realized that during the past few hours they'd been on the road, she'd memorized each knuckle on his long fingers, the shape of the clipped nails and the masculine hair scattered across his tanned skin.

The night of their dinner date, those hands had touched her with real passion. Would he ever touch her again with that same eager longing? She didn't think so. Now when he looked at her she could see he wasn't allowing himself to connect with her on a deeper level. He was being friendly and nothing more.

"Do your parents know about you going to Utah?"

His question interrupted her somber thoughts. "Yes, I called them. Mom was a little concerned until I told her I'd be staying with Maureen's relatives."

His lips made a sardonic twist. "That's stretching things a bit, don't you think?"

"Not really. The DNA proves you're related. We just don't know the how yet." She paused and shrugged. "If we did, I wouldn't be sitting here. I'd be home in Wickenburg, spending my days in the classroom at St. Francis."

His blue eyes slipped over her face. "I've been wondering a lot about why you sacrificed half of the school year just to chase Maureen's dream. It has to be more than your interest in history and genealogy."

She glanced over to the busy street that ran adjacent to the front of the restaurant. But she wasn't actually seeing the traffic. She was seeing herself, miserable and heartbroken.

"It's no deep mystery. Maureen is like a second mother to me. She helped me... Well, after my divorce I was not in a good place, mentally or emotionally."

"What about your parents—your own mother? You couldn't go to them for advice or support? Or were they peeved with you because they'd advised you not to marry Steven in the first place?"

His questions pulled her gaze back to him. "My parents didn't try to sway me one way or the other about marrying Steven. And they did try to help me through the divorce. But ultimately they were too soft with me. Mom would hug me and tell me everything would be okay. Maureen, on the other hand, gave me a firm lecture that included a few curse words about me wallowing in a pity party for myself."

"In other words, she made you face reality."

"Yes." She gave him a wan smile. "She made me see that compared to the rest of my life, Steven was just a tiny blip on the radar."

"So you don't dwell on losing Steven now?"

"Not in the least," she answered in the cheeriest voice she could muster. "So you see, I owe Maureen plenty. Doing this ancestry dig for her is only a small way to pay her back."

"I'll say one thing, Vanessa. You're a loyal friend."

"Maureen helped me," she said simply. "I'm just trying to give back."

"I get it. You're just paying off a debt." He gestured to her partially eaten sandwich. "Better finish your meal. We still have a long way to go."

Jack's father had assured him that the entire family would be informed about Vanessa coming to Stone Creek Ranch long before they arrived. Even so, Jack could only guess at how any of his siblings actually felt about the situation. But he figured none of them would squawk about having an extra boarder in the house.

Whatever their father wanted, he usually got without much of a fuss. That was an unspoken rule of the family. And Hadley wanted Vanessa here on the ranch.

Whether that was good or bad remained to be seen. But as each mile drew them closer to home, the more uneasy he felt. What if Vanessa hated the place and promptly wanted to go back to Arizona? True, Three Rivers was just as isolated as Stone Creek, but that place was so massive it was like a bustling town in itself, and her friends were there.

Why don't you face facts, Jack? What's really

scaring you is the fear that in the next few days your resistance might crumble. You might take Vanessa to bed. And then you'd be a changed man. She'd be in control. Not you.

Trying to ignore the troubling voice in his head, Jack glanced over to see Vanessa had scooted to the edge of her seat and was gazing eagerly at the green valley stretching between two high mesas.

"Jack, this is incredible!" she exclaimed. "It's so wide open and windswept. Are we on Stone Creek Ranch yet?"

"The entrance won't appear for a few miles yet, but we actually entered Stone Creek land a few minutes ago when we crossed over that last cattle guard."

Her wide-eyed gaze swung over to him. "Oh! But you gave me the impression that your family ranch wasn't all that big. This looks huge to me!"

"To most folks, I expect it would seem like a large spread, but compared to Three Rivers it's like a postage stamp next to a highway billboard."

His explanation didn't appear to convince her. She said, "I think you're being deliberately modest now."

"It's best for a man to know his limitations," he replied.

She arched an inquisitive brow at him but didn't press him to explain his comment. Instead, she turned her gaze back to the passing landscape.

"I don't see any trees around here," she commented.

"You won't find trees in this area of the ranch.

Most of the trees follow the riverbanks. And there are some fir and juniper on the higher slopes. We have sage, too, but not as much chaparral or cacti as you have in your part of Arizona."

"Mmm. Well, in spite of being treeless, this green valley is lovely."

The thousands of acres that made up Stone Creek Ranch were all beautiful in different ways, Jack thought. And having Vanessa point out the beauty of this valley made him see it with fresh eyes.

"Maybe you'll have a chance to view some of the ranch before you go home," he said but stopped short of offering to serve as her guide.

He couldn't put himself in a position where the two of them would be completely alone, away from the family and ranch hands. That would be worse than tempting a child with a piece of candy. Before Jack could stop himself, he'd be grabbing for a taste of the sweet treat.

"Someone would have to show me around, and I don't want to make a pest of myself," she said. "I feel bad enough already about putting an extra burden on your mother. But I'll make sure she understands that I can see to my own needs while I'm here."

Someone would have to show her around. She hadn't said *you*. Which made it apparent Vanessa had no intentions of asking him to be her tour guide, Jack thought. He should have felt relieved that he didn't have to make excuses to turn her down. But instead of relief, he felt small and cowardly.

"I imagine Mom is looking forward to having you. It's rare that we have company, and when we do it's usually a rancher come to see Dad about buying cattle or sheep. You're going to be a refreshing change for her."

"I hope so."

After that she remained silent while Jack focused on the winding road that climbed the steep side of a mesa. When the truck reached the flat top, the ranch house below came into view, and Vanessa gasped with pleasure.

"Oh, it's so beautiful!" Then she looked questioningly at him. "This is the Stone Creek Ranch house?"

"That's it," he said and was surprised at the pride he felt.

He glanced at her, and the awed expression he saw on her face made him suddenly realize how much his home meant to him.

Maybe Vanessa has you seeing with your heart now, instead of your eyes. Ever think about that, Jack?

Yeah, he'd thought about the way Vanessa was changing him, Jack answered the troubling voice in his head again. He just wasn't sure the changes were going to be good for him. Or her.

Chapter Eight

Jack parked the truck beneath a tree shading a portion of the front lawn, and after he'd helped Vanessa
to the ground, she walked a few steps onto the green
grass and stared up at the huge two-story house.

The structure had obviously been there for many
years, yet it had been maintained in pristine condition. The outside walls were a combination of large
round rock and lapped-board siding painted a soft
gray that matched the shingled roof. White-board
shutters bracketed the numerous windows on the
front of the house, while at the north end an enormous stone chimney rose high above the roof.

A ground-level porch, covered with the same shingled roof as the house, ran the entire width of the

structure. The space was furnished with four chairs and two love seats, all made of bent willow, while on each end of the porch wooden swings hung from heavy rafters. Pots of red and pink geraniums, along with several ferns, added splashes of color against the gray house.

She was still admiring the view, when Jack walked up behind her, carrying two of her four bags. Since she couldn't guess as to whether she'd be staying a few weeks or several, she'd packed for the latter.

"Let's go in," he invited. "I'll get the rest of your bags later."

"Thanks. I've been too busy looking to remember my bags. I can get what's left."

He inclined his head toward the stepping stones leading up to the front door. "Let's go in and find my parents."

"Okay."

They started across the yard, and Vanessa was wondering why she didn't feel nervous at the prospect of meeting Jack's parents, when the front door suddenly opened and a woman with honey-blond hair stepped onto the porch. Petite to the point of appearing fragile, she was dressed in olive green slacks and a cream-colored blouse that was belted at her tiny waist.

Following a step behind her was a tall, broad-shouldered man dressed in typical denim ranch wear. A black cowboy hat was pulled low over his forehead, but as Vanessa and Jack drew near the porch, he politely removed the headgear and held it down at his side.

"Those are my parents," he said to Vanessa under his breath. "And I'd be afraid to predict what kind of questions they're going to ask you, so be prepared."

She gave him a tiny smile and a wink. "Don't worry. I'm a teacher, remember? I'm good at giving and taking tests."

Jack's parents stood close together in the middle of the porch, and as Vanessa and Jack walked up to them, she noticed Hadley's arm was affectionately hugged to the back of his wife's waist. Jack had told her that his parents' relationship wasn't the same as Maureen and Gil's wildly romantic love match, but it was easy to see this couple were very close. They were also an exceptionally attractive couple, Vanessa decided.

Claire's long hair was slightly threaded with silver streaks and coiled gracefully into a loose twist at the back of her head. Her porcelain complexion held only a few little wrinkles near the corners of her mouth, while her brown eyes twinkled with happy energy. As for Hadley, she saw distinctive characteristics in him that reminded her somewhat of Gil. He had the same tall, muscular build, thick salt-and-pepper hair that waved away from his face and vivid blue eyes that matched Jack's and Chandler's.

Claire was the first to speak. "Jack, you can't imagine how happy I am to have you back home."

"That's an understatement," Hadley said jokingly.

"While you've been gone, all I've heard is Jack, Jack, Jack."

Claire playfully scowled at her husband. "True, but I'd hate to tell him how many times I heard you say I wish Jack was here."

Chuckling, Jack went to his mother and kissed her cheek. "Hello, Mom. It's good to be back home," he said gently, then turned to shake his father's hand. "Dad, it doesn't look like my being gone has hurt you any."

Grinning, Hadley patted his flat midsection. "I can still work you boys down on any day."

Jack turned to Vanessa. "He's telling the truth about that," he told her, then cupping a hand beneath her elbow, he urged her closer to his parents.

"Mom, Dad, this is Vanessa Richardson. Most of her friends call her Van. But I call her Vanessa. I think it suits her better. But maybe she should tell you what she'd like for you to call her."

"Oh, I'm not particular," Vanessa said. "Van or Vanessa is fine with me."

Claire exchanged a shrewd look with her husband, before she turned a smile on Vanessa. "Hello, Van. Ever since Hadley told me you'd be coming to stay for a while, I've been looking forward to meeting you."

Vanessa reached for the woman's hand and found it to be small and delicate with skin as soft as a baby's. When Jack had told her his mother didn't do outside work on the ranch, he hadn't been kidding, Vanessa thought.

"Thank you, Mrs. Hollister. I'll try not to be a bother, I promise."

"Nonsense. It's going to be a joy to have you. And call me Claire," she insisted.

"I will. And thank you for being so gracious about me barging in like this," she told Jack's mother.

"You're hardly barging in, young lady. I told Jack to get you up here even if he had to twist your arm," Hadley spoke up. "I'm glad to see you're not wearing a plaster cast on either arm."

"You're going to learn that Dad is a jokester," Jack told her. "So don't pay attention to half of what he tells you."

"Especially when it concerns Jack," Hadley added teasingly, then held his hand out to her. "Happy to have you here, Vanessa, and thank you for coming."

"Hello, Mr. Hollister. It's a pleasure to meet you."

Smiling, the rugged rancher simply held on to Vanessa's hand rather than shake it.

"Call me Hadley. We're going to be working together, and we're going to be friends. Right?"

His comment sounded so very much like Jack that she couldn't help but smile. "I'm sure we are," she told him.

Jack cleared his throat. "Well, I'll go get the rest of our bags. Mom, do you have a room made up for Vanessa yet?"

"It's all ready. We've fixed a bedroom in the room

I used as a nursery years ago. It's small, but it does have its own private bathroom." She gently placed a hand on Vanessa's shoulder. "Come along, Van, and I'll show you to your room. And then we'll have something to drink."

Vanessa followed Claire into the house, and as the two of them walked down a short foyer, she said, "From what Jack told us, you've been staying at Three Rivers for the past few weeks. I hope you'll find our home as comfortable."

They stepped into a large living room furnished with a mixture of chairs and sofas upholstered in dark green leather and rust-colored fabric. The floor was wood parquet and the walls a warm beige. Low tables were scattered throughout the pieces of furniture, most of them holding lamps, framed photographs and other whatnots. Along one wall, there were several wide windows that faced the north. With the drapes and blinds open, Vanessa could see distant snowcapped mountains.

"Claire, your house is beautiful. I assure you I'll be more than comfortable. But I would like for you to promise me one thing."

The woman glanced guardedly at Vanessa. "Oh. What is that?"

Vanessa said, "That you'll let me do for myself. I'll take care of my own laundry and tidying my room. Oh, and I can cook a bit, too. So if you happened to need help in the kitchen, just tell me. I'll be happy to pitch in."

Surprise flickered in the woman's eyes, and then a gentle smile crossed her face.

"I don't know what to say," Claire said. "I expected you to be mannerly. But I wasn't thinking… Well, you're just a delightful surprise, Van. I mean that. You wouldn't be offended if I gave you a hug, would you?"

Laughing, Vanessa reached out and hugged Claire's shoulders. The physical contact gave her a slight indication of the woman's delicate frame, and she marveled that Claire had given birth to eight healthy children.

When Claire finally stepped back and smiled at Vanessa, her eyes were misty. "We're going to be great friends. I can already tell."

"I'd like that very much," Vanessa told her.

Claire took her by the hand. "Come along and we'll go upstairs. That's where your room is. I wanted to put you next to the twins. I thought you'd feel more comfortable being close to the girls. But I didn't have an empty room next to theirs, so you're going to be between Jack's and Flint and Quint's rooms. I hope you don't mind. If it's any assurance, they're both quiet. Actually, Flint and Quint are both mostly gone at night. Flint is a county deputy, you see, and his hours are sporadic, and Quint—well, he's a socializer. As for Jack, he's a homebody, but he's not much for watching TV or listening to music. He's mostly a reader. That is, when Hadley doesn't have him hooked up from early morning till midnight."

After passing through a wide hallway, they reached a staircase that curved up to the second floor. They climbed it to the top when a door to their left opened, and a very young woman stepped out. She had long blond hair much the same color as her mother's. It was wrapped in a loose bun atop her head, while silver hoops dangled from her ears. A flowing white maxi skirt and a red tank top covered her tall, willowy figure. Yet it was the guarded look in her blue eyes that that caught the majority of Vanessa's attention.

Claire said, "Bonnie, this is perfect timing. I want you to meet Van. She's the young lady who's going to connect the dots on our family tree."

The woman shut the door behind her, then turned back to them. "Hello, Van. Welcome to Stone Creek."

"This is Bonnie. She's a twin to Beatrice," Claire said by way of introduction. "They're the babies of the family."

"Mom, we're twenty-four now," she protested in a soft voice. "Hardly babies."

Shaking her head, Claire directed a hopeless look at Vanessa. "One of these days she'll understand that mothers never entirely quit thinking of their children as their babies."

Vanessa reached her hand out to the young woman. "Hi, Bonnie. I hear you keep the ranch's books. I imagine the job keeps you very busy."

Bonnie's handshake was little more than sliding her fingers alongside Vanessa's.

"It does keep me busy. But I like it," she said, then asked, "Do you plan on staying long, Van?"

"It all depends on how my research goes. But I hope it's long enough for us to get to know one another," Vanessa added warmly.

Bonnie's gaze dropped to the floor. "Yes. That would be nice. Now, if you'll excuse me, I need to get back to the office. I'm expecting a call."

Claire ruefully watched her daughter hurry toward the staircase. "Don't let her attitude put you off, Van. It's nothing personal. Bonnie is very shy. That's one reason she likes working here at home. So she doesn't have to deal with strangers."

"Oh, I'm sorry. Has she always been so shy?"

Claire sighed. "No. It started when she entered her teens. We think it's because Beatrice was always so outgoing. By the time the girls reached high school, Bea was already very popular with her peers. She was constantly being chosen for parts in school plays, a place on the cheerleading squad and a queen or princess for this or that. The more popular Beatrice became, the quieter Bonnie grew. Of course, those school days are long over. But now—well, Bonnie just wants to hang in the background."

"Hmm. Competition between sisters isn't uncommon. But it's a whole different issue when it comes to twins. There's usually a love-hate bond between them that's hard to understand."

"Oh, you sound as if you know children. Do you have some of your own?"

Vanessa shook her head. "No children or husband. But I'm a schoolteacher, and I've had twins in my classroom more than once. Dealing with them can be trying, that's for sure."

Claire touched the back of Vanessa's arm to urge her on down the hall. "A teacher... That's like being a mother to dozens of children."

"Yes. But it's not the same as having your own."

There must have been a wistful note in Vanessa's voice, because Claire gave her an encouraging smile.

"I wouldn't fret over that, Van. You're a lovely young woman. Some fine man will come along and give you a family."

Claire had no way of knowing that Vanessa wished that the *fine man* could be Jack. Or that knowing he wanted no part of having a family with any woman had left Vanessa's heart feeling cold and heavy.

"Perhaps. Someday," Vanessa murmured.

Later that night as a portion of the family sat around the dinner table, Jack wondered if his mother was purposely trying to torture him. She'd sat Vanessa in the chair to his right and Cordell to his left. Sandwiched between the two had Jack feeling like a third wheel or, at best, a moderator.

Jack wasn't the least bit surprised to see Cordell attempting to monopolize Vanessa's attention. His younger brother was more than a flirt, he was a womanizer. He enjoyed having a woman in his life until he grew bored and decided he needed a new one. Even a woman as beautiful and intelligent and sweet as Vanessa could never keep Cordell's heart or hands off the next woman who caught his eye. And Jack had no intentions of seeing Vanessa fall prey to his brother's charm.

"We were beginning to worry that Jack might want to stay on indefinitely at Three Rivers," Cordell said to Vanessa. "Every time he called he was talking about how fabulous the ranch was and how much he liked everyone. Now that I've met you, Van, I can see why he was enjoying the place so much."

Jack purposely pressed his elbow into Cordell's ribs. "Lay off, Cord. Vanessa isn't used to your sleazy kind of talk."

Cordell's jaw dropped. "Sleazy? I didn't say anything close to sleaze."

The look of feigned innocence on Cordell's face made Jack want to give his brother's rib cage another hard dig. "Okay. So you didn't. Just lay off."

From his chair at the head of the long oak table, Hadley said, "Boys, let's not argue in front of Van. You're going to make her feel uncomfortable."

Jack stabbed his fork into a piece of roasted potato. Uncomfortable, hell. He was sitting here in misery, pretending that Vanessa was only a friend.

Why are you fighting with yourself, Jack? You don't have to keep a wall erected between you and

Vanessa. You don't have to stop touching her, kissing her. You could find the courage to take her into your arms and show her how you really feel.

"Well, I want to hear about this other Hollister family," Beatrice spoke up from her seat next to Bonnie. "What are they like? Do they look like us?"

Beatrice's comment broke into the taunting voice in Jack's head, and from the corner of his eye, he could see Vanessa's fork was paused halfway to her mouth as she looked across the table at Beatrice.

"In my opinion, I think your father resembles Gil," Vanessa answered. "He's the head of their family. And Jack favors one of Maureen and Joel's sons. They have the same hair color and blue eyes. I'll tell her to send some photos so that you can see for yourself."

"Yes, Maureen has already promised to send us a few photos," Claire said, then reached over and lovingly patted the top of Hadley's hand. "I can't imagine another man looking as handsome as you, dear."

Hadley chuckled as he gave his wife a pointed look. "If you think I'm going to give in about getting a new couch for the den, forget it. The one we have is fine. Especially when Quint props his dirty boots on it."

Thank goodness Quint had taken off to town tonight, Jack thought. Exposing Vanessa to him and Cordell together would've been hell.

The thought had barely had time to go through Jack's mind when Cordell said, "That's damned spooky. All these years and we didn't know we had family connections in Arizona."

Vanessa said, "Well, Jack can tell you that they're all nice people. They're generous and easygoing and very down-to-earth. You wouldn't know they're worth millions."

Beatrice gasped and Cordell's eyebrows shot straight up. Even shy Bonnie looked up from her plate.

"Millions!" Beatrice said in an awed voice. "Dad, did you know these people were rich?"

Hadley reached for his water glass. "I became aware of their monetary worth after Maureen first contacted me. But none of that has anything to do with us. We have what we have, and they have what they have."

"I'd like to know how we're actually related to these people." Bonnie looked to Vanessa for answers. "Do you have any idea, Van?"

"Not yet. Although it's fairly obvious that it goes back several generations, we just don't know how many. That's why I'm here. Hopefully I can find some information on your grandfather and great-grandfather."

"Good luck," Beatrice said sarcastically. "What we know about those two would fit in your eye. Sometimes I think they must have been outlaws and kept their personal information hidden. Especially Great-grandfather. I've never even seen a picture of him."

"That's a thought, sis," Cordell spoke up and then let out a hearty laugh. "Van might do well to check old prison records here in Utah. Maybe they housed a Peter Hollister."

Jack shot his brother a dark look, but it wasn't enough to wipe the grin from Cordell's face.

"Cord, this is a serious matter," Claire admonished her son. "It isn't a time for joking."

"Who's joking?" Cordell replied. "Dad doesn't know much of anything about his grandfather. Peter could have been an outlaw. Who knows?"

"Outlaws and millionaires," Beatrice repeated sardonically. "Next we'll be hearing there were murderers in the family."

"I don't know of anyone being a murderer yet. But there actually was a murder in Gil's family," Vanessa told her. "Gil's brother, Joel, who was Maureen's first husband, was murdered several years ago."

For once, Jack noticed Beatrice looked a little shamefaced. "Oh, sorry. I was just joking. I didn't know something like that had happened for real."

Vanessa said, "Jack has been told the whole story, so I think it would be best for him to tell you about it sometime."

Beatrice looked eagerly to her brother. "How about now, Jack? This is getting interesting."

"No, Bea," Jack said firmly. "Not at the dinner table. This is Vanessa's first evening here. I think you can find happier things to talk about. Like one of your boyfriends, for instance?"

"Oh, please," Bonnie muttered under her breath. "Let's not ruin dessert."

From his seat at the end of the table, Hadley said, "Van, if you're getting the urge to jump up and leave the room, Claire and I won't blame you. I'm sure you're wondering how you're going to tolerate listening to this for very long."

Vanessa smiled warmly at Hadley. "Honestly, no. I've been wondering what it's like around the dinner table when your other two sons and daughter are here. Does it get any better than this?"

Jack noticed every eye turned on Vanessa before Hadley let out a loud laugh. "That's a good one, Van. I do believe you're going to fit in with this bunch."

Claire rose to her feet. "Now that you kids have ruined Van's chance to enjoy my pot roast, we might as well have dessert. Bonnie, will you be kind enough to help me serve?"

Jack put his fork down and pushed back his chair. "Don't bother with any for me, Mom. I'm full. Thanks, anyway. The pot roast was great."

He stood and as he turned away from the table, he caught a glimpse of Vanessa's face. She looked surprised by his abrupt departure, and so did his father. But Jack wasn't about to pause and try to explain. How could he? He didn't know what was wrong with him. He only knew that the time he'd spent at Three Rivers had changed him. Being with Vanessa had changed him. And now that he was home again, nothing felt comfortable or the same.

The Jack Hollister he knew was gone, and he didn't know how to get him back. He only knew he needed to go somewhere quiet and try to clear his mind.

Nearly a half hour later, everyone had finished eating, and the twins began to carry leftovers and dirty dishes into the kitchen.

"I can help with this," Vanessa said to Claire. "If someone will just show me where to put things in the kitchen. Or I can load the dishwasher."

Shaking her head, Claire gently took Vanessa by the arm and led her out to the hallway.

"Vanessa, I understand you want to do your part," she said. "But tomorrow will be soon enough for you to help with kitchen chores. Right now there's something else I'd much rather you do."

Curious, Vanessa said, "I'd be glad to, if I can. What is it that you're wanting me to do?"

"Go find Jack and check on him. He's not feeling well."

Vanessa tried not to visibly stiffen. Of all the things Claire could've requested, she might have known it would involve Jack.

"You think he's sick?"

Claire gave the side of Vanessa's upper arm a reassuring pat. "Not physically. I'm sure the long drive has tired him. But there's something else… Just go find him. I'm sure it will do him good to talk with you. My son has gone through a lot of changes since he's been away. I can see that, even if his father can't."

Vanessa's heart ached at the thought of Jack feeling mixed-up or hurt. More than anything she wanted him to be happy. Because she cared about him deeply. Perhaps too deeply.

"But Claire, Jack doesn't need my company. He's home with all of you now."

Shaking her head, Claire said, "That's exactly why he needs *you*. Being back with all of us has, well, overwhelmed him."

To look at Claire, she was the exact opposite of Maureen. But Vanessa decided that the two women were exactly alike in one important way. They both had a keen understanding of their children and what each of them needed to make them happy. Only on this occasion Claire was wrong about Jack's needs.

Biting back a sigh, she said, "Okay. I'll check on him. Do you have any idea where he might be?"

Clearly relieved, Claire said, "Down at the old barn, most likely. That's where he usually goes when he wants to be alone. It's a fair distance from the back of the house. But the yard lamps light the path from here to there, so you won't need a flashlight to see your way."

My dad says I'm nocturnal and can see like a cat.

I imagine you've saved plenty of money by not having to buy flashlights.

The words she and Jack had exchanged when she'd taken him on the night hike to the rock hill suddenly came back to her. So did the sweet aware-ness she'd felt at holding his hand and having his lips moving against hers. That night, hope had begun to flicker inside her. The hope that real love was about to come to her. Now she had to wonder if she'd been a fool over a man for a second time around.

"I'll get my jacket and go look for him," she told Claire.

Five minutes later she was walking on a dirt-packed trail away from the house and up a gentle slope. Some fifty yards ahead stood a large barn with a loft and a loafing shed built over one side. Even from a distance Vanessa could see the board walls were a faded red and the roof constructed of corrugated iron with a few rusty patches here and there. A short distance to the left of barn, a smaller shed made of the same material housed a pair of tractors and a long flatbed trailer. For hauling hay most likely, she thought.

Although there were a few wooden corrals erected next to the big barn, Vanessa didn't see any sign of livestock. Unlike Three Rivers, there were no enormous holding pens filled with bawling cows and calves or horses bucking and playing and generally kicking up dust. Nor were there cowboys taking care of nightly chores. This was a quiet place.

She was nearing the open doorway of the big barn when she heard her name called. When she turned toward the sound, she spotted Jack sitting on an octagonal bench built around the huge trunk of a tree.

Why was he sitting there in the dark? This was

his first night home after being away for eight days. Didn't he want to be with his family?

Her mind whirled with the questions as she walked over and took a seat next to him on the smooth, wooden bench.

He asked, "What are you doing down here in the dark?"

"I was about to ask you the same question. And it being dark doesn't stop me from taking a walk. I'm nocturnal, remember?"

The corners of his mouth dipped downward. "Yeah, I guess that had slipped my mind." He glanced past the barn toward the open valley beyond. "If you're looking for a stargazing spot, you won't find it here. The tree limbs hide the sky."

His masculine scent drifted ever so faintly to her nostrils, and as her eyes clung to his somber profile, she wished she had the right to touch him at will. She wished she could cradle his face with her hands and kiss him until his lips were smiling, until the joy of being together was all that mattered.

"I'm not stargazing tonight," she said. "I'll save that for another night. I came looking for you because I…"

"Because Mom sent you. Right?"

The night air had grown chilly. Or was it Jack's distant attitude that was making her shiver? Either way, she pulled the ends of the collar on her denim jacket a bit closer together. "What if she did? Does it bother you that both of us care about you?"

He stared at her in silence for so long that Vanessa finally groaned with sheer disgust.

"Why don't you go ahead and say what you're really thinking, Jack? There's no one else around to hear you. Just me."

His brows pulled together in a scowl. "I'm not thinking anything! Except that I came down here for some peace and quiet. Is that too much to ask?"

Vanessa's back teeth snapped together as she struggled not to curse at him. "Claire had the crazy idea that you needed my company. I tried to explain that you didn't want me around, but she wouldn't listen. See, she thinks that you being her son for thirty-six years has given her insight to your feelings and needs. And she probably does know a lot about you. But not enough. Not like I do. Sorry for the interruption, Jack. Good night."

Without giving him a chance to respond, she jumped to her feet and started back down the trail to the house.

Tears were blurring her eyes, and her breath was coming in angry spurts, when she felt his hand touch the back of her shoulder. Still, she continued striding.

"Vanessa, wait!" His fingers wrapped around the ball of her shoulder and turned her toward him.

She stumbled slightly, and her hands flattened against his chest to catch herself. "Would you kindly let me go? I'm wasting my time out here—with you!"

"We're both wasting time. That much is becoming clear to me."

Her chin came up and she looked at him through tear-glazed eyes. "What are you talking about?"

"This!"

Her mouth opened to speak, but as she gazed at his dear face, every word in her vocabulary vanished. And then his lips came down on hers, and any thought of talking totally slipped her mind.

His kiss was hungry and swift and left her gasping in shocked wonder. "Jack, you—"

"Yes, you don't have to remind me," he said roughly. "I haven't forgotten that I said no more holding you, kissing you. But I no longer give a damn. I've tried to hold fast to my common sense for as long as I could, but I give up. You win."

Amazed, her head turned back and forth. "Win? I didn't know we were having a contest."

"Maybe not in your mind, but in mine I've been fighting a hell of a war."

Anguish twisted his features and made his voice raw. The need to somehow wipe away his anguished thoughts had her reaching up and cupping her palms against the sides of his face.

"Jack, are you troubled to be back home?"

The lines in his forehead grew deeper. "What makes you ask that?"

"A while ago at dinner you seemed aggravated with Cordell."

"I usually am aggravated with Cordell. That's nothing new. But we're tight in spite of that—in spite of everything."

"Oh. I got the impression you might be a bit jealous of him."

Her remark didn't appear to offend him. Instead, he grunted with sardonic humor. "I am. I'm jealous of all my brothers. And they're jealous of me. That's the way it is with us. We're very competitive in everything we do. But we love each other no matter what."

She searched his face for answers. "Oh. Then something else is troubling you," she said.

His gaze dropped to the front of her jacket. "You shouldn't have to wonder, Vanessa. You ought to know what's torturing me. Being cooped up with you in the truck for hours and hours—of having you so close, but telling myself that I shouldn't give in to this crazy desire I have for you."

His moodiness was because of her? It was hard for her to believe she had that much effect on him.

"Do you think any of this has been easy for me? That I haven't been feeling the same frustration?"

Her whispered questions lifted his gaze back to hers. "I don't know. I don't know anything anymore."

"Maybe it's all my fault. I came on to you from the very start. I should be embarrassed to admit that, but I'm not. Because the moment I saw you for the first time, I felt a jolt. And it wasn't just the fact that I found you damned good-looking. It—"

"Stop it! Just stop it!" he whispered as he buried his face against the side of her neck. "I don't want you blaming yourself for anything. I took one look at you and went a little crazy."

His lips began to nuzzle the soft skin of her neck, and with a tiny moan vibrating in her throat, she wrapped her arms around his waist and hugged her body close to his.

"Oh, Jack," she said, her voice thick, "this is the way it's supposed to be with you and me. This is the way it always needs to be."

"I want to believe that, Vanessa."

His lips returned to hers, and for long, long moments he kissed her so deeply that her legs began to tremble, and her lungs burned for oxygen. Somewhere in the far distance she could hear coyotes yipping, then closer crickets chirped a night song.

The sounds seemed foreign to her fuzzy mind, and just as she began to wonder if she'd become lost in a dreamworld, Jack lifted his head and took her by the hand.

"Come over here," he said. "I need to talk with you."

Vanessa was too dazed to question him. Instead, she allowed him to lead her back to the bench beneath the tree.

They sat down close together, and he wrapped both hands around one of hers and pulled it onto his knee.

"Talking about this isn't easy, Vanessa. But I want you to know, and maybe you'll understand me a little better."

Vanessa studied his face. What did he want her to understand? Why he didn't want a wife or children? She didn't want explanations. She wanted to hear him say she'd caused him to have a change of heart. But that was too much to hope for.

"Jack, if this is painful for you, it can wait."

"No, I don't want to wait. Because tonight when you suggested I might be jealous of Cordell...well, I felt like a coward because I couldn't be totally honest with you."

"This is something about you and Cordell?"

He shook his head. "No. Me and Hunter. A few years ago, what happened between us went beyond jealousy."

"Hunter? Where does he come into this?"

He wiped a hand over his face. "He, uh, had the foresight to save me from making a huge mistake. Only, the way he went about it was a bitter dose of medicine."

"I don't get it. When you've talked about Hunter to me, you made it sound like you two are very close."

"We are. I'm closer to him than any of my brothers. But there was a time I literally wanted to beat him to a pulp. Which would've been a mistake for me to have tried," he said wryly. "Hunter is as stout as a bull."

"Something bad must have happened to send you into such a rage."

He turned his gaze toward the shadowy barn. "I caught him with the woman I was planning to marry.

They were, uh…let's just say I couldn't have wedged a thread between the two of them. Get the picture?"

Just knowing that Jack had found his brother making love to the woman Jack was going to marry was shocking. But Vanessa was even more stunned to learn that Jack had once even wanted to get married.

"Very clearly," she said quietly. "So what happened? No—wait, first I think you should explain why any of this took place. Was this woman actually your fiancée at the time?"

He grimaced. "No, thank goodness. But I might have been engaged to her if Hunter hadn't opened my eyes. See, all the time I was dating Desiree, he kept telling me she was no good and I should walk away from her. But I refused to listen. I thought he was just trying to play big, bossy brother and butt into my business."

"Could be you were too in love with this Desiree to walk away," Vanessa suggested, while hating the very thought.

He made a scoffing noise. "It wasn't love I was feeling. But I believed it was. I thought she'd make the perfect wife for me." He made another sound of disgust. "Hunter kept saying she was out for herself. That all she wanted was my money. Not that I have much money to speak of, but I suppose it was more than she had. And people in this area consider us to be well-off." He let out a short, caustic laugh. "With you being friends with the Arizona Hollisters, I'm sure that sounds funny."

"It's not funny at all. Most of us aren't in the same financial league as the Three Rivers Hollisters, Jack. You have nothing to be ashamed of."

"No. Besides, money isn't everything. But Desiree must have thought so."

She studied his somber face and tried to imagine how crushed he must have felt to discover he'd been betrayed. From her own experience with Steven, she knew exactly how deep the humiliation must have stabbed him. She also knew the scars from it never entirely went away.

"So what about Hunter? Was he just playing around with her because she was available and he could?"

"No. He purposely set the whole thing up with her. He'd already tried talking sense into me, so he decided the only way to open my eyes was to show me the real Desiree."

Vanessa looked at him in amazement. "Oh. So you didn't know that in the beginning. You thought your brother had betrayed you, along with Desiree."

He nodded. "Hunter and I had a big fight. But by the next day I could see it all clearly. I told Desiree exactly the kind of woman she was—someone unworthy of my love and trust. Then I told Hunter I'd be grateful to him for the rest of my life."

With a thoughtful shake of her head, she said, "Jack, surely you're not thinking I'm anything like Desiree. That I could be so duplicitous?"

"Hell, Vanessa, that thought never entered my

mind," he said. "You're the exact opposite of her. That's why—with you I know there would be no halfway. It would be all or nothing."

"Meaning?"

He grimaced. "You're not the type for an affair. And I'm not sure I'm ready, or even capable of falling in love. Yeah, while you're here we could have some casual dates. But is that what you really want?"

It wasn't. She knew the more time she spent with Jack, even in a casual way, the more she'd want him. And having a brief affair with him? Yes, it would be exciting, but not nearly enough.

"I understand your thinking, Jack. After the ordeal with Desiree I imagine you've vowed to never let yourself fall for another woman. You don't want to be hurt and humiliated and made to feel like a fool a second time."

His lips slanted into a wry twist. "Okay. Go ahead. Tell me how I shouldn't let one miserable breakup ruin the rest of my life."

"No, I'm not going to lecture you. If I did, I'd have to lecture myself," she said gently. "See, you're not the only one who's been betrayed before. It's tough. But I don't want pity."

He studied her for a long moment, and then his expression softened. "What do you want, Vanessa?"

"You," she said simply.

He sucked in a sharp breath, and then his hands were on her shoulders drawing her to him.

"And I want you. So very much."

His head lowered, and as his lips angled over hers, she wrapped her arms around his neck and let her kiss convey just how hungry she'd been for his touch.

But even as the taste of his lips clouded her mind with pleasure, she knew that kissing him, holding him in her arms, wasn't enough to convince him to open his heart.

Chapter Nine

From a small office on the second floor of the ranch house, Vanessa stood at the window and gazed down at a portion of the backyard. Someone had turned on the sprinklers, and the afternoon sunshine sparkled off the carpet of thick green grass. To one side of the grassy slope, next to a low stone wall, a rose garden created a sea of beautiful blooms of red, yellow, white and pink.

Vanessa had been surprised to discover the rose garden. Not that growing roses was anything peculiar, but it wasn't something that came to mind when thinking of a cattle-and-sheep ranch. And with its stone fence and tall tea roses, this particular garden had a distinctly British feel about it.

Jack had told her the garden had supposedly been planted at the same time the house had been built and that Lionel had been resolute about keeping the roses tended and in perfect condition. For his wife? He'd eventually divorced the woman, but the garden was still there and perfectly cultivated. Had the man's love continued on for his ex-wife or had there been some other woman? Vanessa couldn't help but wonder.

I caught him with the woman I was planning to marry.

These past few days, since Jack had told her about the incident with Desiree and Hunter, she'd thought plenty about how it had undoubtedly shaped Jack's plans for the future. He was full of mistrust. She could understand that much. But he could see that Vanessa wasn't the same sort of woman as Desiree. So why couldn't he trust her?

She hadn't found the courage to ask him that question. Mainly because she didn't want to risk tearing the new bond that had steadily been building between them this past week. Jack was no longer keeping a cool distance from her. To her delight, he was actually getting closer. But the doubtful part of her continued to wonder how long he'd allow this closeness to go on. Until they were completely alone and the chemistry between them exploded? Would he back off again and remind her that they shouldn't get intimate?

The questions were looping monotonously through

her brain when she heard footsteps behind her and then a light knock on the door.

"Van, am I interrupting?"

Vanessa turned away from the window to see Bonnie entering the office carrying a tray with an insulated coffeepot, along with cups and an assortment of flavored creamers.

Happy to see the young woman, Vanessa walked over to greet her. "Not at all. Please come in, Bonnie. How did you know I could use some coffee?"

"By midafternoon I start slumping. I thought you might need a break, too."

"You came at just the right time. I was wasting time standing at the window daydreaming."

She followed the young woman over to a pair of armchairs separated by a small table. While Bonnie placed the coffee tray on the table and began to fill two cups, Vanessa sank into one of the chairs.

Bonnie handed her one of the cups. "I'll let you fix it to your liking."

"Thanks." Vanessa spooned hazelnut creamer into the steaming liquid, then added a good measure of sugar. "So how has your day been going?"

Bonnie eased into the seat next to Vanessa's. "Good so far. The phone hasn't been ringing off the hook. And Dad has only found five items he wants ordered from an online vet store. But the day isn't over. He'll probably find more."

Vanessa had been very surprised on the second day after she'd arrived on Stone Creek when Bonnie had offered to help her carry boxes of old papers and family documents down from the attic. Since then, to Vanessa's surprise and delight, Bonnie had been warm and friendly and nothing like the shy girl she'd first met.

"I admire you, Bonnie. You must have patience of steel to work with your father like you do. Not that Hadley is an ogre. He's a very nice man. So is my father, but I think I'd pull out my hair if I had to work with him. He'd be constantly treating me like a daughter instead of an employee."

"Yes, there are times Dad forgets that about all of his children. But he's not terribly bossy. Not unless he thinks it's necessary." She motioned toward the boxes the two of them had carried from the attic. "Have you been looking through any of that stuff today?"

Vanessa took a sip of coffee before she answered. "I've managed to dig my way through two of the smaller boxes. So far I found a few photos of your grandfather Lionel and his ex-wife, Scarlett. But it's like his father, Peter, never existed. I can't find a photo or any sort of legal document with his name on it."

"I've been thinking about that and wondering what might be the reason there's so little information about him. You know, I recall Dad mentioning something about there being a fire here on the ranch. He was only a boy at the time, but he said it destroyed a few rooms of the house. I'm wondering if that's how some of the family's personal information went missing."

Vanessa's ears pricked up in curiosity. "A fire? That's interesting. Your father hasn't mentioned anything about it to me. I'll run the idea by him and see what he thinks. There's also something else that puzzles me. It's about the roses."

Frowning thoughtfully, Bonnie said, "What about them?"

"They're beautiful. Someone obviously takes great care of them."

"Mom does most of that. Out of respect for Lionel. She says he was a wonderful father-in-law."

"Hmm. He must have been a romantic to have made such a garden for his wife."

Bonnie's brows lifted. "Oh, I don't think it was for her. Lionel told Mom that the rose garden was a memorial to his mother, our great-grandmother. I think her name was Audrey."

For his mother! Bonnie's revelation put a whole different slant on things, Vanessa thought. "Do you know your great-grandmother's maiden name?"

"Not exactly, but Dad probably will. Seems like it was something along the lines of Starbuck or Stanwick. Maybe Starwood. I can't be sure."

A few days ago, she'd met Jack's other brothers, Flint, Hunter and Quint. From the short time Vanessa had been in their presence over dinner, she'd concluded Quint was a bit of a rebel, while Flint was the quiet, serious sort. As for Hunter, each time she'd looked at the man, she'd thought about how he'd deliberately made love to Jack's girlfriend. Still, she'd found him friendly and engaging.

She'd also gotten the impression from the three men that having relatives in Arizona by the same name meant little or nothing to them. Only Jack, the twins and Cordell, to some extent, seemed to have a real interest in the matter. But Vanessa supposed that could change if the how or why was uncovered. As for Grace and her view of the matter, Vanessa hadn't yet met the middle sister of the group.

"Knock, knock!"

Vanessa glanced over to see Jack standing in the doorway. He was wearing a pair of scarred batwing chaps and jingle bob spurs. His black hat was so dusty that at first glance it looked brown. But those things were only a gritty backdrop to his toothy grin.

"Jack, come in," Vanessa invited. "Bonnie and I were just having coffee."

"I see how hard you two are working," he teased as he stepped into the room. "It must be exhausting lifting those heavy coffee cups."

Bonnie practically jumped to her feet. "Uh, I do need to get back to the office. I have work waiting."

"Bonnie, I was only teasing," Jack said, as she whizzed by him on her way to the door.

"I know. But I need to go anyway."

She stepped out of the room and shut the door behind her. Jack walked over to Vanessa and sat down in the chair Bonnie had just vacated.

"I didn't mean to run her off." He shook his head. "Sometimes I never know what to say around her. She's so sensitive."

"You didn't offend her. She wanted to give you time alone with me."

His brows shot up. "Why? You think she knows about you and me?"

What was there to know, Vanessa wanted to ask him. Other than the fact that electricity arced between them each time they got within three feet of each other. Everyone in Jack's family had undoubtedly noticed it by now.

"Yes. I imagine your whole family can see the way we look at each other."

He reached over and wrapped his fingers around hers.

"And how do we look at each other?" he asked gently.

Smiling suggestively, she leaned toward him. "Like two people who want to be together."

"Hmm. If that's the case, then they won't think it odd if you go horseback riding with me tomorrow."

Totally surprised, she said, "Horseback riding where?"

"A herd of sheep needs to be moved. Normally, Quint and a ranch hand handles that sort of task. But I told him a few minutes ago that I'd take care of it this time. For once I made my little brother happy."

"So you and I are going to herd sheep?" She laughed softly. "Jack, when I told you I could ride a horse, that only meant I could manage to keep my seat in the saddle and my feet in the stirrups, and that's about it. I can't chase livestock!"

He chuckled. "Don't worry. You won't have to do anything except keep the horse walking forward. The dogs will do most of the work."

She tilted her head to one side as though she had to carefully ponder his invitation. "It would be nice to see more of the ranch," she said.

"That's my intention."

She squeezed his fingers. "I'd love to go. When should I be ready?"

"About nine in the morning. I thought we'd take sandwiches and have lunch before we come back to the ranch."

Her eyes sparkled. "A picnic? Wow! Sounds like you're planning to treat me."

His blue eyes softened as he took in her wide smile. "I hope to."

"Thank you for inviting me," she said softly.

His fingertips drew lazy circles on the back of her hand. "It was a selfish gesture on my part. To have your company. I want to make up for lost time."

"Lost time?"

His expression turned rueful. "Yeah. For those days I was being an idiot for thinking I could stay away from you."

Just the mention of that strained time between them caused Vanessa's gaze to drop to the pearl snaps in the middle of his chest. "You're weren't exactly being an idiot, Jack. I mean, you knew you were leaving Three Rivers and we'd probably never see each other again. You had no idea that I'd end up coming up here to Stone Creek. You were just trying to be practical. But it…was an awful time for me."

Standing, he drew her up from the chair and, holding on to both her hands, pulled her close. "It was an awful time for me, too, Vanessa. And now, well, nobody has to remind me that you're here on a temporary basis. You'll eventually have to go home to Wickenburg and resume your teaching job. But I don't want us to think about that right now. I want us to enjoy this time we have with each other and let the future take care of itself."

His words weren't exactly what she longed to hear him say. But her time here at Stone Creek with him was too precious to waste on arguments about the future. For now she was going to live for the moment. She was going to grab each opportunity she was given to be with Jack, as though it would be her last. Because one of these days, it would be.

Because Lionel's wife, Scarlett, had hated the dust and noise of a working ranch yard near the house, he'd built another one, a half mile east of the house. Behind a tall hill dotted with sage and an occasional juniper, the sprawling area consisted of two large barns, three loafing sheds and a network of wooden corrals.

With no trees or shrubs growing near the structures, there was nothing to break the wind that swept brutally down from the north during the winter months or to supply shade in the hot summer. But Jack was accustomed to battling the extreme weather. The cold and heat and the changing seasons at Stone Creek were as much a part of him as the land itself. For the rest of his life, the ranch would be his home.

But what about Vanessa? Her home is in Arizona. Her life is there with her job and friends and family. She'd never leave it for you. Yeah, Desiree would've taken your marriage offer because you could've given her more than what she had. But Vanessa already has everything she needs, and it isn't you, Jack.

The critical voice drifting through his head caused him to pause in the act of tightening the girth on the horse he was saddling and lift his gaze to the distant mountains. He couldn't deny that having Vanessa on the ranch was a sweet blessing. Just being in the same room with her made him happy. And yet in the moments he allowed common sense to step into his thoughts, he saw himself as a fool deliberately standing in the middle of a railroad track, hoping against hope that a train would never come.

"Hey, brother, as far as I can see, there's nothing over on Snow Mesa. You're wasting your time if you're expecting to see a bison or antelope or even a rangy coyote wander across the range."

At the sound of Cordell's voice, Jack shook away his dark thoughts and finished tightening the girth.

He said, "I'm not expecting to see any wildlife. I was…thinking about things."

Cordell led a blaze-faced sorrel up to the wooden hitching post and wrapped the lead rope securely around the battered wooden rail.

"Oh. What kind of *things*? That damned family tree? If you ask me, it's all a waste. Being related to a group of people down in Arizona doesn't make any difference to our lives. We have plenty of relatives on our mother's side of the family, too. But we rarely visit them. I don't see that being related to another bunch of Hollisters is anything to get excited about."

Maybe none of it did matter to Cordell or his other brothers, but it had already made a hell of a difference to Jack's life. "You wouldn't say that if you knew the Hollisters. And you're wrong. It does make a difference."

"Well, I suppose it has to you," he said as he pushed a heavy brush over the sorrel's back. "You met Vanessa."

Jack didn't bother asking his brother what he meant by the remark. Like Vanessa had said, the whole family could see how Jack looked at Vanessa and how she looked at him.

"Yeah," Jack replied. "Vanessa is…special."

Cordell folded his arms against his chest. "What do you plan to do about her?"

Jack pushed the end of the leather girth strap into

the keeper on the saddle before he turned to face his brother.

"You would ask such a question. Think about it, Cord. I've only known Vanessa for a few weeks. If you're expecting to hear wedding bells ringing for me, you're delusional."

With a mocking grunt Cordell pushed the brim of his hat up on his forehead and leveled a pointed look at Jack. "Am I? And here I was thinking you'd finally come to your senses and put that business with Desiree out of your head."

Jack muttered a curse word. "You know darn good and well that she's been out of my head for years now."

"Okay, I didn't phrase that quite right. It's not Desiree that's in your head, it's the deceitful way she treated you. Maybe you'd better work on cleansing your mind of that before you make any decisions about Vanessa."

Jack scowled at his brother. "Maybe you'd better keep your nose out of my private life, Cord. I don't exactly see you making a family for yourself."

Cordell let out a caustic laugh. "No. And you won't, either. But you're not like me, Jack. You're a good guy. And Vanessa has eyes for you. I'd hate to see you make a mistake and let her get away."

It wasn't unusual for Cordell to bring up the subject of women with Jack. Actually, women were probably his favorite thing to discuss. But it was highly unusual for Cordell to get serious on the matter.

Jack drew in a deep breath and blew it out. "Trust me, Cord, I don't plan on making a mistake with Vanessa or any woman."

Jack untied the mare's lead rope and led her over to the horse trailer hooked behind his truck. Cordell strode along at his side.

"What's the deal with two horses and the trailer?" he asked. "I figured you were riding over to the west range to check on the heifers."

Swinging the back door of the trailer open, Jack jumped a dark brown horse into the compartment and tied him safely to a crossbar before he replied to his brother's comment.

"I'm taking Vanessa on a ride. We're going to move the north sheep down the canyon to better grass."

"Well, that's more like it," Cord said with a clever grin. "Take your good easy time. I'll take care of things here. I've sent Quint and the men out to repair that cross fence over by the meadow. He's not happy, but what the hell. He's never happy, anyway."

Jack stepped out of the trailer and reached for the mare. "Quint is still young. He hasn't yet figured out who he is."

Cordell snorted. "Don't you mean our youngest brother hasn't learned to appreciate what he has? Sometimes I think Dad ought to kick his butt off the place."

Jack paused to look at his brother. "Would that make you feel good?"

Grimacing, Cordell scuffed the ground with the toe of his boot. "Guess not. But something needs to wake him up. He doesn't want to take orders from me or Dad."

Jack cut him a wry glance. "Hmmph. Did you want to take orders when you were twenty-six?"

Cordell chuckled guiltily. "No. But I kept all the complaining to myself."

"Most of the time," Jack reminded him.

Cordell stood to one side while Jack loaded the mare into the trailer and secured the back gate behind both horses. But as he started to climb into the truck to leave, his brother stepped up to the door.

Jack started the engine, then leaned his head out the open window. "Was there something else on your mind, Cord?"

"Nothing urgent. I only wanted to say…well, I shouldn't have said what I did a few minutes ago about the other Hollisters, about being related to them not making any difference. I didn't mean to sound like a jerk."

"Forget it. I already have."

The sheepish expression on Cordell's face turned to open curiosity. "Are they really as nice as you say? You think I'd like them?"

So Cordell wasn't as indifferent as he'd wanted Jack to first think. He smiled at his brother. "I'd bet all I have in my bank account that you would. Maybe you and I can make a trip down there sometime, and you can see for yourself."

Cordell's expression brightened. "Sounds great, but who'd help Dad take care of this place while we were gone?"

"Hmm. Might be a good way to make Quint step up to the plate," Jack suggested.

Laughing, Cordell lifted a hand in farewell. "Yeah, right. See you later, brother."

Dressed in jeans and boots and a brown felt hat that Bonnie had kindly loaned her, Vanessa was ready and waiting when Jack braked the truck to a stop in front of the ranch house.

As she walked out to meet him, she noticed with a bit of surprise that he was leaving the saddled horses inside the trailer.

"Good morning, Vanessa," he greeted her with a sexy grin. "Ready to sling your leg over the saddle?"

Laughing lightly, she made an vague gesture to her denim shirt and jeans. "I'm dressed for it. But the real question is, can I *stay* in the saddle?"

"Sure, you can." His gaze traveled appreciatively from her boots to the top of her head. "I have every confidence in you. And wearing a hat like that, how could you fail?"

Smiling, she touched the brim of the battered hat. "Bonnie was sweet enough to let me wear hers."

He curved his arm against the back of her waist and urged her toward the truck. "I'm surprised to see how my sister has taken to you. She doesn't make friends with just anybody."

"I'm glad we've become friends. She's a special young lady."

"Maybe having you around will help her believe in herself."

And what about him? Vanessa wondered. Would he begin to believe they were meant to be together? Or was he still seeing Desiree in the arms of his brother?

Trying not to dwell on that troubling question, she gestured toward the horse trailer. "Aren't we going to ride the horses from here?"

"No. The sheep are up in the mountains. And it's a half-hour drive to the trailhead. We'll mount up there," he explained.

He whistled for the dogs, and two black-and-white Australian shepherds came racing up from the old barn.

Totally ignoring Vanessa, the feisty animals jumped into the bed of the truck, and Jack fastened the tailgate.

"Since I've been on the ranch, I've tried to make friends with this pair, but they don't want anything to do with me," she told him. "Are the dogs this unfriendly with everyone? Or is it something about me?"

They walked around the truck, where he opened the passenger door for her. "They're working dogs," he explained. "Not pets. They're more comfortable around the sheep than humans."

"Hmm. I'm learning something new around here every day."

He wrapped a hand beneath her elbow and helped her into the bucket seat. "Good things, I hope."

She slanted him a coy look. "Don't worry. Your family hasn't told any bad tales about you—yet, that is."

He chuckled. "I can only hope they keep the bad stuff to themselves."

Once he climbed into the driver's seat, he set the truck into motion, and for the next twenty minutes they traveled north, across a wide valley floor that mostly consisted of grass and sage and black cattle grazing peacefully beneath the bright morning sun.

Eventually the open prairie began to narrow until the valley became little more than a wide gulch. Rugged mountains rose up to the front and sides of them, while off to the left, a shallow creek wound through stands of willows and aspen trees.

The roughness of the trail forced Jack to slow the truck to a crawl, until he finally stopped the vehicle near a stand of gnarled juniper trees. Here the sage stood thick and tall, while farther up on the foothills, pink and yellow wildflowers bloomed among slabs of rock.

As soon as they climbed out of the truck, Jack lowered the tailgate, and Vanessa watched in amazement as the dogs immediately shot up the mountain and out of sight.

"Jack, they're running off!" she exclaimed. "Aren't you going to call them back?"

"No. They already know where the sheep are. When we reach the herd, they'll be there." He motioned for her to follow him to the back of the trailer. "Come on. Let's get the horses unloaded."

Once the horses were safely on the ground and he'd tightened the cinch straps on both saddles, he handed the gray's reins to Vanessa. "This is Sunflower. She's a sweetheart, so don't worry that she'll get unruly with you. She won't."

Sighing with pleasure, she glanced around her. "I can't imagine the area where we're going could look any more fabulous than this."

A crooked grin on his face, he walked over to where she stood. "Maybe I'd better take a second look around me. I never thought of these mountains as fabulous."

"That's because you're a practical man."

"Practical, huh?" He stepped close enough to curl an arm around her waist. "Well, this down-to-earth guy promises that from here on out, the view will get prettier. But it can't compare to you."

Vanessa's heart pounded as his forefinger came up to touch her cheek.

"That's a lovely compliment, Jack. But it isn't necessary," she murmured. "Just being with you like this is all it takes to make me happy."

He nuzzled his nose against her temple. "Being with you is special, Vanessa. I went to sleep last night thinking about today, of being with you and how it was going to feel to have you to myself. And I woke up thinking the very same thing."

She tilted up her chin in order to look into his eyes. "And how does it feel to have me to yourself?"

"Like I've been handed a Christmas gift in August. The only thing that could make it better is a kiss."

Her smile was deliberately provocative. "What's stopping you?"

Groaning, he trailed his fingers down the side of her face. "If I kissed you now, we'd never get to where we're going. The sheep would never be moved, and Cord would have to pull a couple of men off fence repairs to come out here and do the job you and I were supposed to do."

"Oh my, I had no idea that one kiss could cause such a domino effect."

"In this case it would." He pressed his lips to her forehead, then gently set her away from him. "So let's mount up. The sheep aren't all that far from here."

Vanessa hadn't ridden a horse in several months, and even then the trek had been over flat, smooth ground. She'd never ridden up rough and rocky mountain trails with tree limbs slapping her in the face and the incline so steep that her butt very nearly slid over the back cantle of the saddle.

But she found the challenge exhilarating, along with the view. The higher they climbed, the more she could see of the valley below and a jagged ridge of purple mountains in the far distance.

Every few minutes Jack would stop to look back and make sure she was following directly behind him. And each time he saw that she was managing to keep up with him, he rewarded her with a pleased smile. A sight that warmed her heart.

After ten more minutes of the steep climb, the trail broke over the top, and Vanessa gasped with pleasure as a small meadow stretched before them. At the far end, a fairly large herd of sheep was bunched into a tight circle.

"I wasn't expecting this!" she exclaimed. "And just as you said, the dogs are with them."

"And that's where they'll stay until I tell them we're ready to go."

"Did you train them?" she asked.

"No. Cordell does that. We have another pair of dogs over at the ranch yard just like these, except they're brown-and-white. We mostly use them to help round up cattle." He motioned for her to follow him into the opening. "Come on. I know a nice little spot to eat our lunch."

They rode across the meadow to where a small grove of fir trees grew among an outcropping of rocks. In the cool shade, Jack dismounted, then walked over to where Vanessa was carefully climbing down from the saddle.

"Better let me give you a hand," he said, as he wrapped his hands around her waist.

"I can make it. I—" Her words halted as her feet hit the ground and her knees promptly threatened to buckle beneath her. "Oh! My legs have turned to rubber!"

Chuckling, he anchored his arm around her to prevent her from falling. Vanessa was grateful for his help. She was also very aware of his closeness and the warmth of his arm radiating through the denim to heat her flesh. What would he do, she wondered, if she turned and wrapped her arms around him? If she lifted her lips up to his? Tell her it wasn't the right time? That they still had a job to do?

"That was a long ride for a novice," he said. "You made it like a real pro."

Deciding she didn't want to take the chance of being disappointed, she eased away from his hold and, with a good-humored groan, rubbed her buttocks. "You got the novice part right. But I'm fine now, Jack. Let's find a place to sit and eat."

He pointed to a stand of rocks. "Over by the boulders," he suggested. "There's a thick bed of pine needles there. It should be a comfortable spot. I'll get our lunch."

While he went to fetch his saddlebags from the horse, she headed over to the rocks, but halfway there, she caught something glimmering in the corner of her eye. Fascinated, she walked beneath the canopy of pine boughs until she arrived at a tiny pond. The smooth water was clear and partially surrounded by small boulders. Sheep and other wildlife had made deep tracks in the soft dirt near the pond's edge. To the far right of the watering hole, low-growing bushes were covered with some type of berries.

"Jack," she called over her shoulder. "I just found our dessert. Huckleberries!"

She was plucking a handful of berries when he walked up behind her. "August is the month huckleberries are ripe for picking. Don't tell Mom. She'll send us back up here to pick them. She likes to make huckleberry jam."

Vanessa popped a couple of the berries into her mouth. "Hmm. That might not be so bad. Especially if she lets us eat some of it."

Clearly amused, he took her by the arm. "Come on. We'd better eat before you ruin your appetite."

They returned to the spot by the boulders, where he'd left the saddlebag and a canteen. Vanessa sank down on the soft pine needles and rested her back against the tall boulder. Jack sat down next to her and proceeded to pull sandwiches from the leather bags.

"If you think we need a tablecloth, I can undo my slicker from the back of the saddle," he offered as he handed her a thick sandwich wrapped in clear plastic.

"I'm perfectly fine like this." She let out a contented sigh. "It's so quiet and lovely here. The only sounds I hear are the birds and the wind in the pines. It's like we're miles away from civilization."

He slanted her a wry grin. "That's because we are."

"You know, seeing what I have of the ranch today, I understand why Hadley is so proud of it. And why he obviously wants his sons to keep the legacy going."

He pulled out another sandwich for himself and a hard plastic container filled with potato chips. "Yes, in that way, Dad is a lot like Gil."

But where would the legacy of Stone Creek end up, she wondered, if none of his sons had children? Maybe Jack didn't think the ranch was worth tying himself to a woman and children.

The notion left a bitter taste in her mouth, and she bit into the ham and cheese sandwich in hopes the food would wash it away.

"So tell me, what do you do with the sheep here at Stone Creek?" she asked after she'd swallowed the bite of sandwich. "Sell them for meat?"

He shook his head. "When Lionel was still alive I believe he sold some of the sheep for meat. But once he died and Dad took over running the ranch, that stopped. For one thing, Mom detested the idea of the lambs ending up on someone's dinner table. She put her foot down and told Dad to either raise the sheep to sell the wool or get out of the business entirely."

"So Hadley agreed to just raise them for wool," she said thoughtfully. "I'm glad that your mother stuck to her guns. And your father thought enough of her to go along with her wishes. But to be honest, I was as surprised as the Three Rivers Hollisters to learn that you raised sheep. Your grandfather must have had a fondness for them."

"Apparently. Dad said when he was a kid, the ranch probably had a couple thousand head or more. Now we're down to about five hundred. Cattle take up the most of our grazing land. Which makes more sense. That's where we make our money. Wool is profitable only if you're able to sell it at special markets."

She ate a few more bites of sandwich before she asked, "Do you do the shearing yourselves?"

"No. We contract professionals to do that. Shearing takes place in the spring, and it makes for a busy time on the ranch."

She looked over at him, and as her gaze traveled slowly over his rugged face, it was impossible to imagine not ever knowing him. Loving him.

Love? The word had come out of the blue and hit her before she'd had time to think. No! She hadn't fallen in love with Jack, she argued with herself. There hadn't been enough time for her to lose her heart to him. There had to be another reason why she wanted to throw her arms around him and never let go.

Suddenly a tight lump formed in her throat and turned her voice husky. "I'd like to see the shearing. But I'll be long gone by springtime."

He didn't reply, and Vanessa remained quiet as she forced herself to eat the last of her sandwich.

After a long stretch of silence, he said, "Yeah,

guess you'll have to go home to Wickenburg in December."

Her mind recoiled from the very idea. Which was stupid. She couldn't stay here with him forever. Not unless he miraculously fell in love with her. And she couldn't foresee anything like that happening.

She drank from the canteen, then placed it on the ground between them. "At the pace I'm making, I won't have anything solved by Christmas." Fearing the hopelessness she was feeling might show on her face, she purposely turned her head away from his probing gaze. "And your parents didn't sign on for a permanent houseguest."

"I wouldn't be worrying about Mom and Dad. They don't care how long you stay at Stone Creek."

She swung her gaze back to his face, and something in his eyes made her heart thud with anticipation. And before she could stop herself, she asked, "What about you, Jack? Do you care?"

He pushed aside the canteen that was lying between them and then scooted close enough to pull her into the circle of his arms.

"What do you think?" he whispered.

Her arms slipped around his neck and brought her lips next to his. "I think I want you to make love to me. Now. This very minute."

A groan rumbled deep in his throat. "Vanessa, you don't know what you're asking of me."

She eased her head back just enough to look into his eyes. "Yes, I do. It's simple. I'm asking you to become a part of me. I'm asking you to let me become a part of you."

"Simple. Yes," he whispered.

And as his lips came down on hers, Vanessa closed her mind to everything but his kiss.

Chapter Ten

Nothing had changed between them, Jack thought, as he tightened his arms around her. The more he tasted her lips, the more he wanted. And the deeper he took the kiss, the more she responded.

It took less than a second for their mouths to fuse hotly together, their tongues to intertwine. The intimate contact sent desire slicing through him like a bolt of lightning, and before he recognized what had hit him, his brain turned to fog, and his manhood hardened with aching need.

With his arms wrapped tightly around her, he continued to kiss her with a hunger that shocked him. He hadn't known it was possible for him to want this much. Need this much.

He was wondering how this reaction had happened, when he felt their bodies listing sideways. Without breaking the contact of their lips, he placed his hands on her shoulders and lowered both of them to the ground.

The pine needles were a soft cushion, and the pungent aroma mixed with her flowery scent to create a swirling mist that carried him away to a place he'd never been.

When he finally found the will to ease his mouth from hers, he buried his face in the curve of her neck and tried to gather his senses. But they were already too scattered. And why did he need to think now, anyway? Vanessa was holding him, caressing him, asking for his love. This was the very thing he'd been craving since the moment he'd met her.

"Jack, do you know how much I want you?" she whispered against his cheek. "How long I've wanted to be with you like this?"

Lifting his head, he looked down at her and the soft, wondrous look in her eyes caused something in his chest to swell until he thought it was literally going to take his breath away.

"Vanessa. Sweet, sweet, Vanessa. This isn't the way it should be," he said with a rueful groan. "You should be lying on sheets. Not pine needles."

Her hands slipped to the front of his shirt and began to unfasten the pearl snaps. "I'm lying right where I want to be. With you. That's all that matters to me."

In a saner moment, he would've argued with her. He would've told her they needed to wait until they were in a soft bed with a roof over their heads. But he was past being sane, and he was tired of waiting, tired of fighting himself.

"I don't deserve you."

Smiling gently up at him, she pulled apart the last snap on his shirt. "I probably don't deserve you, either. But here we are. And it feels pretty wonderful to me."

Her hands slipped beneath the parted fabric and slid warmly over his flesh. The contact was like a hot branding iron searing permanent marks on his skin.

"Yeah," he said thickly. "Pretty wonderful."

He lowered his mouth back to hers and kissed her until he was on the verge of exploding with the need to have his body connected to hers.

Apparently she must have been feeling the same desperate need. As soon as he broke the contact between their lips, she whispered, "I think it's time we got undressed, don't you?"

"Past time," he agreed, while reaching for the front of her shirt.

She brushed his hands away and pushed herself to a sitting position. "Let me do it this time. It'll be faster."

This time. How many more times was she planning on this happening? How many more times could his heart endure it? The wild questions raced through his mind as he began to peel his shirt from his shoulders. But by the time he'd removed his boots and jeans, the only thought in his mind was making love to her.

When he turned back to her, she was already lying naked beside him, and for a long moment all he could do was stare at her in amazement. In all of his life, he couldn't remember seeing anything more lovely. The lush curves of her hips and breasts, the strands of her black hair brushing against brown puckered nipples, the satiny glow of her olive skin, everything about her came together to form perfection in his eyes.

He breathed her name as his hand reached out and cupped the weight of one breast. "I was wrong when I said you couldn't get any prettier. You're incredible."

She took his other hand and placed it on the opposite breast. "No. What's incredible is having you touch me."

With his hands caressing both breasts, he leaned in to her and kissed her, gently at first and then with a hunger he couldn't contain. And all the while her hands were racing over chest, down his arms, across his back, then onto his buttocks.

It wasn't until he felt her hips arching into his that a brief slice of sanity slipped into his thoughts, and he sat straight up.

"What's wrong?" she whispered.

"I, uh, I just now thought about...protection."

"I'm on the pill, Jack. It will be okay."

Nothing would be okay if he made Vanessa pregnant! But she wouldn't see it that way. No, she was a romantic. She only thought about love and all that went with it.

His brain partially froze at the thought, but it wasn't enough to cool the fire in his loins. Nothing but having Vanessa's body next to his could douse the coals simmering deep in his gut. "That…might not be enough. I have a condom in my wallet."

She didn't say anything, and he quickly went about finding the packet and putting it on. However, when he turned back to her, she had a clever little smile on her lips.

"Good thing you came prepared."

Jack rarely blushed, but her words were enough to send a hot rush of color over his face.

"Vanessa, if you—"

He broke off the rest of his sentence as he spotted the soft, pleading look in her eyes.

"Oh, Jack," she murmured hoarsely. "Don't say any more. Don't make me keep waiting."

She held her arms out to him, and Jack didn't wait around for a second invitation. He stretched out beside her and pulled her into his arms.

With his fingers delving into her silky hair, he pressed his cheek to hers. "For a second there, I thought you were going to jump up and run off."

She linked her arm around his waist and turned her face just enough to match her lips to his. "Not a chance. I have you where I want you, and I'm not letting go."

Groaning, he covered his lips with hers and eased her onto her back. The kiss quickly carried him away, and as his lips plundered hers, his hands began a hungry foray of her plump breasts, the indention of her waist and the flare of her hips.

Her skin was smooth and soft and deliciously warm beneath his hands. And though he hated to give up the sweetness of her lips, the need to taste her skin lured his lips to the side of her neck.

She moaned as he nuzzled his way down to her shoulder, then onto the delicate collarbone and finally the sweet center of her breast.

As soon as his lips wrapped around the budded nipple, her hands dove into his hair and anchored his head to her breast. Jack lathed it with his tongue, then gently sucked the bud between his teeth.

By then Vanessa was arching the juncture between her thighs against his rigid manhood. The contact very nearly made him lose control, and he swiftly lifted his head.

"Are you ready for this, Vanessa? Truly ready?"

"I've been waiting for you—for this—all my life," she whispered urgently. "I'm so very ready, Jack."

There was no doubt or hesitation in her voice, only longing, and the sound tugged at something deep within him. So deep that it caused his hands to tremble as he took her by the shoulders and pulled her beneath him.

But it was far too late to wonder about the upheaval going on in his heart. Her hands were already clamping a hold on the sides of his waist, drawing him down to her.

Slowly and gently Jack joined their bodies, and as her warm softness surrounded him, his mind went blank. All he knew was that Vanessa was beneath him, asking and giving and filling him with incredible pleasure.

"Vanessa."

With her name on his lips, he lowered his head and their mouths melded together in a hot, hungry union. At the same time, she matched the thrust of her hips to his, and then everything became a wild, incredible blur. He couldn't touch her enough, taste her enough. The pleasure inside him became so intense it turned to a red-hot ache.

Above his head, the breeze whispered through the pine boughs, and farther away, the sheep bleated. The horses stomped and switched their tails at an occasional fly. But Jack heard none of these things. All he heard was a wild roaring in his ears and the faint moans coming from Vanessa's throat.

It wasn't until she cried out his name and tightened the hold she had on his rib cage that he recognized their journey was coming to an end. And though he tried to hold back his climax, it was too great to stop. In the next instant he was whirling and floating high above the mountaintops, and Vanessa was there with him. Safe in his arms. Forever.

* * *

So that's what making love was supposed to be. That's what all the fuss was truly about, Vanessa thought dreamily. It had taken years and meeting Jack to finally learn how it felt to give every particle of her being to a man.

With a sigh of contentment, she opened her eyes and discovered that her cheek was lying against his damp chest. Beneath her ear, she could hear the rapid thump of his heart, and the sound was as precious to her as that of his quick, ragged breaths.

"It's fitting, you know, that we don't have a roof over our heads."

His fingers meshed into the hair at the back of her head. "It is? Why?"

His voice held a raspy note as though he'd been asleep for a long time and was still trying to wake.

"Because an open sky seems to work as an aphrodisiac on you," she said.

He pressed his lips to the top of her head. "Just like I need an added temptation around you."

She sighed and trailed her fingers down the side of his ribs. There wasn't an ounce of extra flesh anywhere on his body, and Vanessa thought she could spend hours touching him and exploring the hard slopes and hollows. Unfortunately, they didn't have hours to spare.

The thought caused her to rise up on her elbow and gaze down at him. Sweat still dampened his forehead and the dark strands of hair hanging near his brows, while his eyes were half-closed.

The urge to lean down and kiss him was strong, but for the moment, the question running through her mind far outweighed the yearning.

"Jack, I realize it's rather late to be asking, but... are you regretting this?"

His eyes suddenly opened, and his blue gaze locked onto hers. "Regret? After what we just shared I couldn't feel regret. Why are you asking me?"

"Because I..." She hesitated as a mixture of joy and uncertainty flowed through her. Maybe she was asking because, as wonderful as the experience they just shared was, she couldn't help wondering if he simply viewed it as sex. "Uh, I only wanted to know if I'd disappointed you in some way."

Frowning now, he rose to a sitting position and wrapped his hands around her shoulders. "You're crazy to even ask that question. You were incredible—everything I could want and more. Does that answer your question?"

No. It answered very little, she thought. Because the real question she wanted answered, and what she desperately needed to hear, was whether he loved her. Yet it was becoming increasingly clear to her that he had no intention of bringing up the four-letter word. And neither would she. At least, not today. But sooner, rather than later, she had to know how he really felt about her.

She could feel her lips trembling as she gave him

the best smile she could muster. "Sure. You've answered."

He pressed a soft kiss against her forehead, then frowned as he spotted the pine needles stuck to her bare arms and back.

"So much for a bed made by Mother Nature. Stand up, and I'll brush you off so that you can dress."

Disappointment caused her jaw to drop. "Can't we stay here just a bit longer?"

His eyes widened slightly. "Is that what you want?"

Suddenly, all that mattered was having this time with him last a bit longer. As for what might be going on in that heart of his, she'd worry about that later.

Wrapping her arms around his neck, she nuzzled her cheek to his. "Yes. I want this. You."

With his hands gently cupping her jaw, he brought her lips around to his. "I think the sheep can wait awhile longer," he murmured.

By the time Jack and Vanessa moved the sheep from the mountaintop to a lower meadow located a mile away, then rode back to the truck and trailer, afternoon shadows were growing long across the valley floor. Luckily, the only chore he had left for the day was tending to the horses.

As Jack steered the truck over the last of the rough track leading to the ranch house, Vanessa quietly stared out the passenger window at the passing landscape.

On one occasion, she'd pointed out a herd of antelope grazing close to the river, and then a second time she exclaimed over spotting several mule deer bounding through the sagebrush. But other than that she hadn't said much, and her silence made him wonder what was going on in that pretty head of hers.

No doubt she was tired. The day had been long, and they'd ridden over some very rough terrain. Even so, he wasn't sure that her quietness had been brought on by fatigue. It was more like she was preoccupied, and he wondered if she might be growing homesick. Or was she merely sick of trying to figure out his way of thinking about the two of them?

What the hell difference does that make, Jack? And why are you wondering about Vanessa's silence? You haven't said more than five words to her since you started back to the ranch house. At least, not the words you should be saying to her. But no, you're too much of a coward to open your mouth now.

Coward. Stupid. Selfish. The self-descriptions had been whirling around in Jack's head like a revolving door that couldn't be stopped. Yes, if he was any kind of a stand-up man, he would've told her that she was the most wonderful thing that had ever happened to him. He would've admitted that he wanted her to be with him for the rest of his life. But that would be the same as confessing that he loved her. And he wasn't ready for that. No. He wasn't ready to hear her say she cared about him and she was enjoying her stay on Stone Creek, but her home and job were in Arizona. Her parents and friends were there. Her life was there. He couldn't expect her to uproot just to have a long-term affair with him.

Affair, hell. She wants love, Jack. Think about that.

"I see the ranch house in the distance," she said.

Thankfully, her comment managed to push aside the voice in his head, and he glanced over to see she'd straightened her back and was peering through the windshield.

"Yes. I'll let you out and then take the horses on to the ranch yard."

"No need for that," she told him. "I can help you deal with the horses."

"Thanks, but I can take care of them," he said more gruffly than he intended. "I'm sure you'd like to rest a bit before dinner."

She darted a perplexed glance at him. "Okay. If you insist. I do need to clean up. And Maureen is expecting me to call her this evening. I should do that before dinner."

"You've told me that you talk with her every day. Is that necessary?" he asked, then seeing her brows pulled together he quickly added, "Sorry. I should've asked if you *wanted* to talk with her that often?"

"Well, yes. I do. Because she started all of this. She deserves to know if I've made any headway. And anyway, I like hearing how things are at Three Rivers. Especially with the new babies."

This morning when Vanessa had talked about

Hadley eventually handing the reins of Stone Creek over to his sons, he'd thought about the Arizona Hollisters and how there were plenty of generations being born to carry Three Rivers forward and into the far future. But with Jack's family, Grace's six-year-old son, Ross, was the only child who'd been born into the family so far. He and any children that his twin sisters might have could certainly end up working the ranch, but it was up to Jack and his brothers to keep the Hollister name going.

Babies. Oh yes, the idea of him and Vanessa with a baby had entered his thoughts before and after he'd made love to her. And the notion had left a bittersweet taste in his mouth. It had also made him wonder if he could ever be like Holt and Blake, or Chandler and Joseph.

"Yes," he said. "I need to remember that your home and loved ones are down there. Have a nice chat with Maureen and tell her I said hello."

From the corner of his eye he could see her lips part as though she was going to say something, but she didn't. Instead, she reached for the backpack she'd brought with her and waited for him to brake the truck to a stop in front of the house.

Before he could make a move to help her down from the cab, she opened the door and quickly jumped to the ground.

"Sure, I'll tell her. See you at dinner," she said, and with a little wave she turned and hurried toward the house.

"Yes. See you then."

Jack watched her stride gracefully to the porch and then enter the house, and all the while, he wondered what was happening to him and to her. He could feel everything between them changing, and he didn't know how to stop it or if he should even try.

The next morning, Vanessa was in her office, sipping a cup of hot coffee and sifting through a stack of old orders and receipts, when Hadley knocked on the door and stepped in.

"Good morning, Hadley," she greeted.

"Don't worry, I'm not going to pester you for very long." Smiling, he pulled off his cowboy hat and sank into one of the chairs sitting in front of her desk. "I'm on my way to Spanish Fork, but Bonnie mentioned that you wanted to speak with me about something."

"Oh, yes. Last night at dinner it slipped my mind, or I would've mentioned it then."

"Hmm. Well, with Hunter showing up for dinner, none of us could get a word in edgewise. The guy's life is too busy. That's why he's divorced. But that's a whole other story in the life of my children."

Yes, Hunter had monopolized most of the conversation, but that had mostly been because his siblings had wanted to hear about his latest travels. However, Jack had remained so quiet during the meal that Claire had eventually remarked on his behavior. But Jack had simply explained it by saying that he'd had a long day.

Later, Vanessa had wanted to ask him if having sex on the mountain had exhausted him that much, but she didn't have the chance. Shortly after everyone had left the dinner table, he'd disappeared. Sometime after she'd gone to bed, she'd thought she'd heard his bedroom door open and shut, but she didn't bother to look. It had been obvious to Vanessa that he'd wanted to be alone, and she'd decided it was probably best to let him have his wish.

Biting back a sigh, she tried to push Jack out of her mind and focus on Hadley. "Well, thank you for stopping by, Hadley. My question for you is about the fire that happened at Stone Creek when you were a child. Bonnie made mention of it, and we were wondering if any part of the house burned that might have held personal information about your father or grandfather."

Frowning thoughtfully, he rubbed a hand against his jaw. "Hmm. You know, that fire hasn't crossed my mind in years. Frankly, I can't remember much about it. Except that it didn't seem all that major at the time. It started in the kitchen, I think, and spread to two other rooms. I recall some of the ranch hands and my parents fighting the blaze. But they ran me and my brothers totally out of the house. After they managed to put out the flames, there was soot and nasty water everywhere. Dad had carpenters come in and rebuild."

"I see. Well, what were the two rooms next to the kitchen that were damaged?"

He shook his head. "One was Scarlett's sewing room. The other room I remember was where Dad sat in a big leather chair and drank whiskey and read books. Reading and drinking were two of his favorite things to do."

"Hmm. Well, if he had books in that particular room, there might have been other things like papers and documents that might have gotten damaged or destroyed," Vanessa suggested.

"Could be," Hadley said, then looked at her with sudden dawning. "Say, now that we're talking about the fire and all it destroyed, I remember something I should have thought of earlier. When I was older, before my parents divorced and Scarlett, uh, left the ranch, I remember one day I walked in on a conversation they were having. For some reason she was asking my father about his birth certificate. Why, I can't tell you. But I remember him being short with her and telling her that his birth certificate was none of her business."

"That's odd. Why wouldn't he want his own wife to see the document?"

Hadley shook his head. "Anybody's guess. You would've had to have known my parents to understand. They didn't share much about their lives. Dad was the stern, no-nonsense sort, and Scarlett was a bitter woman who always thought someone owed her something. They never got along, and to be honest, Van, it was a relief when they divorced and Scarlett moved out of our lives. My brothers and I no longer had a mother, but at least there was peace in the house."

On more than one occasion, Jack had mentioned that his family hadn't always been as loving and united at the Arizona Hollisters. Maybe that was an added reason he didn't want to be a husband or father, Vanessa thought.

"I understand. So have you ever seen your father's birth certificate? Perhaps he never had one," she commented.

"No. When Dad died we looked for one but gave up trying. And then, as you know, Claire and I made another search while Jack was down in Arizona."

"Well, I'm going to write to the Department of Health and Statistics here in Utah and see if they can send me a copy," Vanessa told him. "It would be a big help to have his exact birthdate. As it is, I'm fishing in the dark."

"I should have done that years ago," Hadley told her. "Just never seemed to have a need until Maureen started this relative thing."

Vanessa gave him a reassuring smile. "I'll handle it. That's what I'm here for."

He regarded her for a long moment, then said, "I hope you know how happy Claire and I are to have you with us. You've brought a little extra life to the house."

"Thank you, Hadley. I've been enjoying every minute. Just don't let me wear out my welcome."

He batted a hand through the air. "We want you

to stay as long as you'd like. In fact, I think I can say that for all the family."

...guess you'll have to go home to Wickenburg in December.

When Jack had made that comment, he hadn't asked if she'd be willing to stay here with him, to make her life here with him. But why would he? After the way he'd shunned her last night and this morning, it was evident that yesterday was just a sex romp to him. He could get the same thing from any willing woman.

"I hope so," she said quietly.

Another moment of silence passed, and then Hadley rose to his feet and levered his hat back onto his head. "Time's ticking. I'd better be going. Uh, there is something else. Do you have any idea what's wrong with Jack?"

The question caused her insides to momentarily freeze. "Is something wrong with him?" she asked in the most innocent voice she could conjure.

"Must be. I imagine you noticed how he hardly spoke at dinner last night. And this morning he left before daylight without saying anything. I thought... I know you went with him yesterday to move the sheep. Did anything go wrong between you two?"

Vanessa could only hope that from where Hadley was standing, he couldn't see the warm blush stinging her cheeks. "If it did I wasn't aware of it. I tried to be a help to him, but I've never ridden much or herded any kind of livestock. I imagine I got in the way more than I helped."

Actually, up until they climbed into the truck to start the drive home, Vanessa had believed everything between them was wonderful. But he'd gradually seemed to slip into his own thoughts, and the closer they'd gotten to the ranch house, the quieter he'd grown. She'd tried to figure out what might have come over him and had wondered if she'd inadvertently said something that might have upset or offended him. But she couldn't think of anything she'd said or done. Except make love to him. And in the end, she'd decided that was the only thing that could be bothering him. He was suffering from a bad case of remorse.

"That sort of thing would never bother Jack." Hadley walked over to the door, then glanced back at her. "He must have something else on his mind. Forget that I asked. Whatever is wrong, he'll snap out of it. Sometimes he's just too damned sensitive."

What would Hadley think if he knew what had really gone on between Vanessa and his son? she wondered. He wasn't a judgmental man. But he clearly wouldn't want his son to get mixed up in a messy relationship.

She took a sip of coffee to ease the tightness in her throat. "I've noticed Jack studies long and hard about things."

"Sometimes a man can study too long. Sometimes

he just needs to do rather than ponder," Hadley said. Then lifting a hand in farewell, he went out the door.

Once Vanessa heard his footsteps move down the hall, she lowered her head and rubbed the middle of her forehead. Yesterday for a few incredible hours, she'd thought her dreams might actually be coming true.

Now she could see how stupid she'd been to let her hopes get so carried away. Just because Jack had given in and had sex with her didn't mean he was thinking of her in a permanent way. And just because his touches and kisses had felt like real love to her, that didn't make them real.

"Jack, we've had to put up this fence at least four times in the past six months," Cordell said as he gestured to a section of sagging barbed wire. "Cross braces might help. Or do you think it needs the whole thing replaced? We're talking nearly a mile. A big expense. And on top of that, you have the gorge to deal with."

Jack did his best to focus on Cordell's question, but instead of seeing the span of sagging wire, he was seeing Vanessa's black hair spread upon the bed of pine needles and the alluring tilt of her lips as she'd held her arms out to him.

A little more than a week had passed since that day he'd made love to her. And just as he'd feared, the passionate union had shifted everything in his mind and his heart. Now he was torn between common sense and a hopeless longing he couldn't shake.

Cordell snorted. "Hell, Jack, would you wake up? I didn't drive us all the way out here to Snow Mesa just for you to stare off in space."

Giving himself a mental shake, Jack looked at his brother. "I was just thinking."

Cordell rolled his eyes. "Obviously."

"About the fence," Jack said flatly. "As much as I hate to think of the expense, sending men out here to fix this one is costing us in other ways. We need to start over with a new one. Double the stretch post and the line posts."

"What do you think Dad will say?"

Jack blew out a heavy breath. "Don't worry about Dad. He understands the expenses of ranching. Come on, let's get back to the ranch yard. The vet is supposed to come look at Nosey. After that trek in the mountains, he's picked up a limp in his left front."

Cordell glanced shrewdly at Jack. "Looks to me like you've picked up something worse than a limp."

Jack didn't reply to his brother's dry assumption until the two men had climbed into the cab of the work truck. "Your name should have been Nosey instead of my horse."

"Oh, come on, Jack. I'm not being nosy." He started the truck and turned it in the direction of the ranch yard. "I'm being a concerned brother. Ever since you took Vanessa to move the sheep, you've turned into a walking zombie. And she's like a ghost around the place. The only time she appears is at the dinner table, and even then she doesn't eat. She just sits there and cuts her eyes toward you while Mom and Dad do all the talking. This nonsense has been going on for a week. I don't know what's wrong, but whatever it is you damned well need to fix it."

Jack's first instinct was to yell at Cordell and tell him to mind his own business. But biting his brother's head off wouldn't help anything. It would only make Jack feel worse.

He heaved out a heavy breath. "I know you're concerned, Cord. But I don't know how to fix it."

Cordell shook his head. "I'd say you better figure it out and quick. 'Cause I'm thinking Vanessa isn't going to stay around here much longer."

Jack's head jdeerked toward his brother. "Why? Have you been talking to her?"

Cordell smirked. "Calm down. I haven't been talking privately to her. It's just an impression I'm getting."

Jack picked up his leather gloves lying on the bench seat and absently slapped them together. "She came up here to Stone Creek for Dad's sake," he muttered. "Because he asked her for help. She didn't come because of me."

Shrugging, Cordell said, "Okay. Then, there's no need for you to worry about anything, is there?"

"No," Jack said bluntly. "Nothing at all."

Chapter Eleven

That same night, after an awkward dinner sitting next to a somber Jack, Vanessa decided she had to do something.

This past week, she'd been waiting and hoping that Jack would come to her and explain his behavior, at the very least give her a reason as to why he'd been avoiding her. But he hadn't. And each day that passed with him exchanging little more than polite small talk with her, the angrier she grew.

Last night she'd finally managed to corner him in the den, where she'd asked him outright as to why he'd been avoiding her. But he'd given her a lame excuse about being overworked and tired, then made a quick escape before she could question him further.

The whole thing was ridiculous, she thought. On the mountain they'd been as close as any two people could get. The memory of having his naked body next to hers, of feeling him moving inside of her, was still so fresh in her mind, to think of it was like pressing a hot iron to her flesh. And she couldn't continue to bear the pain.

Everyone in the house had retired for the night when Vanessa left her room and walked down to Jack's door. Seeing light coming through under the door, she tapped her knuckles lightly against the wooden panel.

After a brief moment, the door swung open, and Jack stood staring at her as though she'd arrived from some other planet. He was wearing a pair of old jeans but no shirt, and his feet were bare. From the looks of his tousled hair, he'd already been in bed or he'd been raking his fingers through it.

"Vanessa, what are you doing?"

"I'd like to talk with you. May I come in?"

The hesitation on his face told her he wasn't keen on the idea, but to her relief, he pushed the door a bit wider and stepped to one side.

Vanessa walked past him and into the bedroom, where a lamp on the nightstand shed a golden glow on a portion of the bed and the wooden floor that stretched beneath it.

"Couldn't this wait until morning? It's getting late. And anyway, it wouldn't look good if someone walked in."

Infuriated that he would use that childish attitude with her, she walked back over to the door and clicked the lock. "There. No one can walk in now. Feel better?"

His lips pressed together. "I'm thinking about you. And what my family might think."

She moved across the floor until she was standing in front of him. "I'll tell you what they'd think. That I'm a grown woman, and if I want to visit you in your bedroom, then I should."

A muscle in his jaw jumped, and then he stepped around her and walked over to a pair of windows. The drapes were open, and beyond the glass Vanessa could see a cluster of twinkling stars hanging over the distant mountains.

An open sky seems to work as an aphrodisiac on you.

Too bad she couldn't lead him outside right now, Vanessa thought glumly. Maybe then he might want to hold and kiss her, tell her how wrong he'd been to keep a cold distance between them.

"I know why you're here. You want to know why I've been avoiding you. Yeah, I have. I guess I should apologize for not having the guts to explain my feelings to you. But I thought you'd get the message on your own and understand."

"Oh, I do understand, Jack." She walked up behind him but stopped short of touching him. "You were lying to me all the time. And I've been so gullible and stupid that I believed you."

His head twisted around to look at her. "Lying? When have I ever lied to you?"

Suddenly the pain in the middle of her chest was so great, she could scarcely breathe. "When I asked you if you regretted making love to me, you said you didn't. But your behavior this past week speaks the truth."

Groaning with frustration, he turned to her. "I wasn't lying, Vanessa. I haven't regretted that day. You gave me more pleasure than I ever knew I could feel. But later, it dawned on me that I was doing you wrong. Each time you looked at me, I knew you wanted to hear me say things that... I just couldn't say. I couldn't give you false promises. That would've been even worse. So I—"

"You just ignored me like I was a rug or something you could just disregard," she said angrily. "Look, Jack, I've never expected a bunch of flowery promises from you. I got those from Steven, and they were as hollow as a rotten log. All I want from you is honesty. If you don't want me to be a part of your life, then tell me flat out, and let me go about forgetting everything that's happened between us."

His eyes were like two chunks of ice as he stared at her, and then like the instant flare of a match, she saw a spark in the blue depths. And suddenly his hands were on her shoulders, drawing her straight into his arms.

"You want me to be honest, Vanessa, then I will

be. I've been aching and sick without you—without this!"

Before she could utter a word, his mouth came down on hers, and then speaking became unimportant. All that mattered was the feel of his lips plundering hers, the heat of his hands roaming over her back and clamping her bottom.

As the kiss grew hotter, his fingers reached for the buttons on her blouse, and Vanessa didn't question his intentions. He obviously wanted her as much as she wanted him, and for the moment that was the only thing that made sense to her bruised heart.

Hardly two minutes passed before they were both undressed and lying together on his bed. And just as quickly, Jack wasted no time in parting her legs and entering her with one smooth thrust.

Her cry of pleasure was muted by his kiss, and then he began to move inside her. Slowly at first, then quicker, until the room began to whirl around her and everything became a blur of sensations pouring over and through her.

The end came as fast and furiously as it had started, and when he finally rolled away from her, they were both panting and drained.

Jack was the first to make a move, and Vanessa watched through half-closed eyes as he sat up on the side of the bed and raked a hand through his hair.

No cuddling next to his warm body, she thought. No soaking in the afterglow of being loved.

Because you're not loved, Vanessa. If you didn't know that before, you certainly do now.

The no-nonsense voice in her head gave her the strength to sit up and reach for her clothing. As she zipped up her jeans and buttoned up her blouse, she tried to gather the right words to say to him. But nothing she said now could convey what was in her heart. Besides, she could see that he wasn't ready to hear that she loved him. Moreover, she had to face the bitter fact that he'd never be ready.

"I'm sorry, Vanessa. I didn't mean for that to happen," he said, then shook his head with regret. "No. That's not true. I did want it to happen. When I'm near you, my willpower is worthless."

His remark made her furious.

"I understand, Jack. You didn't want any of this to happen between us," she said bitterly. "You didn't mean to have sex with me that first time when we went to the mountains. But don't feel guilty. I'm the one to blame. I'm the one who's been the big fool in all of this for thinking you might actually care about me—about us!"

He pulled on his jeans and shirt, then walked over to where she stood at the end of the bed and as his hands wrapped over her shoulders it was all she could do to keep from pulling away from his touch and lashing him angry words.

"Vanessa, you deserve more than me. You deserve the husband and children you want. And someday when you get them, you'll be glad I didn't try to hang on and ruin your life."

Didn't he understand he'd already ruined it? she wondered. Didn't he know that it would be impossible for her to settle for any other man now that he'd been in her life?

"Maybe so, Jack." Turning, she did her best to smile at him, but her lips quivered with the effort. "I only want you to be happy. So don't worry. I won't be making any more trips to your bedroom or to the mountain or anywhere else with you. From this point on, the two of us are nothing but acquaintances. You see, I've decided the best thing I can do for both of us is to go home to Arizona. So you can breathe a sigh of relief and get back to the life you had before I came around and messed it all up."

Shoving her tousled hair off her face, she held her head high as she walked out of the room and quietly closed the door behind her.

Vanessa slept very little that night, and the next morning she tried to hide the dark circles beneath her eyes with makeup before she walked into Hadley's study. But Jack's father was eagle-eyed, and she figured he was going to take one look at her and know something was amiss.

"Good morning, Van. Have you had coffee yet? Claire just brought me a whole pot." He gestured to a wall table where a tray held a thermal pot and coffee fixings.

"Thank you, Hadley, but I've already had a cup at breakfast." She walked deeper into the room. "Do you have a moment to talk? I don't want to interrupt anything."

"I have all the time in the world for you. Please, sit down. In fact, I'm glad you came by. I was just wondering if you'd received anything in the mail about Dad's birth certificate."

Feeling like a traitor, or worse, she sank into a chair positioned in front of his desk. "Nothing yet. And I... Well, I hate to tell you this, Hadley. You and Claire have been so wonderful to me and I—I've really come to love it here, but I'm going back home to Wickenburg. Tomorrow. That is, if you can find someone to drive me to the airport. I've already made a reservation for a flight out of Cedar City."

Disappointment swept over his face. "You're leaving? But why? I thought you were happy, and the genealogy search is just getting underway."

"I'm sorry. I'm hopeful that you can find another person to figure out the ancestry mystery. One that can make more headway than me."

Shaking his head, he said, "I don't give a damn about that. The family tree will all come together in due time. It's you that I care about." His eyes narrowed shrewdly. "Is this about Jack? Is he chasing you away? And don't try to tell me there's nothing between the two of you. I may have a little gray in my hair, but I'm not so old that I can't see sparks in my son's eyes."

Vanessa couldn't hold back a sigh. "Jack and I... His wants in life are different from mine. He belongs here at Stone Creek, and I belong back in Arizona. It's that simple."

He shook his head. "From the look on your face, I don't believe anything about your decision is simple. But since you've made up your mind, I'll see that someone is ready to drive you to Cedar City in the morning."

Bending her head down, she tried to swallow away the lump of tears in her throat. "Thank you, Hadley. I appreciate you. More than you know."

Suddenly he was standing behind her chair, and his big hand was gently patting her shoulder. The consoling gesture caused tears to pour from her eyes, and before she could stop herself, she jumped to her feet and buried her face against his broad chest.

"Aw, little lassie, don't cry. Everything will be okay. You just trust me."

Except for one light hanging over the horse's stall, the barn was dark. The ranch hands had left hours ago, and no doubt the family had already consumed dinner and gathered in the den for coffee. Normally, Vanessa would be there, and so would Jack. But not tonight. He figured she was in her room, packing for her trip home.

Home. Why did a part of him keep thinking Stone Creek was her home? Why was the thought of never seeing her again tearing him right down the middle?

"Jack, what are you doing here in the barn at this time of night? Is Nosey's foot still giving him problems?"

At the sound of Hunter's voice, Jack turned away from the stall to see his older brother striding up to him.

"Nosey is better. The abscess busted, and Chance has been soaking the foot twice a day. What are you doing here at the barn at this time of night? I didn't know you'd made it home."

Hunter eyed him shrewdly. "Is that why you weren't at the dinner table tonight? Because you thought I wouldn't be there?"

Jack shrugged and focused on the shadows beyond his brother's shoulders. "No. I just wasn't hungry."

"Oh. Well, it's probably best that you missed it. The whole bunch acted like they'd taken sedatives. Mom even looked close to tears. What's the matter with everyone, anyway? I was afraid to ask."

Jack turned away from his brother and wiped a hand over his face. "I didn't realize the family cared that much about her," he murmured more to himself than to Hunter.

"Who? What are you talking about?"

Jack slanted him a dejected look. "Vanessa is leaving. Going back to Arizona."

"What? You mean she's already solved the family-tree thing?"

"No. This has nothing to do with the ancestry

business," he said dully. "She's leaving because of me. We, uh, have some differences. The kind that makes it awkward for both of us."

Hunter stared at him in disbelief. "And you're going to let her go? Jack, you're a bigger fool than I ever thought. First you think you want to marry that no-good Desiree. Now you finally have a once-in-a-lifetime chance to have a good woman in your life, and you're going to let her slip away!"

"What the hell do you expect me to do?" Jack blasted at him. "Her home is in Arizona. Her teaching job is there. So are her parents and friends. I can't ask her to give all that up for me."

"Why can't you? If she loves you—"

Jack interrupted before Hunter could continue. "She's never mentioned anything about loving me—"

"Knowing you, I don't imagine you've mentioned it to her," Hunter said slyly. "And I could be all wrong about this, but maybe you don't care if she leaves. Because you don't love her."

The last threads of Jack's composure snapped, and with a guttural groan, he turned his back to Hunter. "Why don't you go ahead and twist the knife a little deeper?"

Hunter sighed and then rested his hand on Jack's shoulder. "Flint and Quint called me a bastard for the way I exposed Desiree to you. But I don't care. I didn't feel guilty then. And I don't feel guilty now. I loved you too much to see you make such a mistake. That's why I'm twisting the knife—again."

Jack swallowed hard. "You can't fix a coward, Hunter. And that's what I am. After the debacle with Desiree, I lost all my confidence about women. I had no desire to get within ten feet of one. But then I met Vanessa, and something happened to me. I was drawn to her. And then suddenly the Hollisters were pulling me into their lives. They all have wives and babies and happiness, and I thought how I'd never have those things. But I couldn't help but want them anyway."

"Why can't you have them? Vanessa doesn't want a family?"

"That's the problem. She wants a husband and family. But I'm not sure I can be what she wants. I'm not even sure she loves me enough to become my wife."

A moment of silence passed, and then Hunter said, "You're probably thinking I'm the last person to be giving advice on love and marriage. Mine ended in divorce. But when a man makes mistakes, he usually learns from them. The way I see it, you have to take a chance and ask Vanessa how she feels about you. Otherwise, you'll never know what you might have lost or could've had."

"Yeah," Jack said in a raw voice. "Better to lose trying than to lose from doing nothing."

Vanessa was taking one last look around the bedroom when Hadley knocked on the open door.

"Your bags are all loaded, Van. You probably need to get going. Otherwise, you might miss your flight."

From the moment she'd climbed out of bed this morning, tears had been burning her throat and eyes. Now that it was time for her to actually leave, it was a real fight to keep them at bay.

"I was just making sure I hadn't left anything behind, Hadley." The room looked bare, yet she felt sure she was forgetting something. Like her heart. But it wasn't here among these four walls. No, her heart was with Jack, wherever he was. She hadn't seen him since she'd walked out of his bedroom. Which was probably a good thing. Facing him now would only crush what was left of her.

She walked over to where Hadley was waiting by the door. "I'd like it very much if you'd walk out with me."

Smiling gently he held his arm out to her. "I wouldn't think of letting you go without me."

Thankfully, Vanessa had already said her good-byes to the rest of the family. Hadley was the only one left, and as he walked her out of the house and down to the waiting truck, she realized she had grown very attached to the big teddy bear of a man.

"Well, I guess this is goodbye," he said. "It's been a joy having you. I hope you'll come back to see us—soon."

"I'll try. One of these days I might surprise you and just show up out of the blue."

She kissed his cheek, and he opened the truck door and handed her up into the seat.

"Goodbye, Van. Safe travels."

After he shut the door, Vanessa expected him to step back and wave her off, and she was somewhat surprised when he promptly turned and walked back into the house.

The sound of the driver's door opening brought her gaze around, and she stared stunned as she watched Jack climb into the driver's seat.

Her voice squeaked with disbelief. "What are you doing?"

He twisted the key and, after clicking his seat belt in place, put the truck into motion. "I'm driving you to Cedar City," he answered bluntly.

"Is this some sort of joke? Your father promised he'd have someone drive me. I can't believe he chose you for the job!"

"Everyone else was busy." He braked the truck to a stop and darted a glance in her direction. "Would you rather cancel your reservation and wait until someone else can drive you?"

No. To delay the inevitable would be just as torturous as riding the next ninety miles with him.

Staring straight ahead, she said, "No. All I want is to get to the airport on time."

"Then, snap your seat belt together, and I'll get you there," he said curtly.

She did as he asked, and as he drove away, she

steeled herself against the urge to gaze back at the beautiful old ranch that had briefly been her home.

Except for a few words exchanged about the weather, the thirty-five-minute drive over the rough, graveled road to Beaver passed mostly in silence. But once they passed through the small town and headed south on the smooth highway, Jack seemed to relax, and to her amazement began to talk about the ranch and the work they'd been doing the past few days.

"No one has probably mentioned this to you, but I haven't been able to ride Nosey. Not since we came back from moving the sheep."

Surprised, she looked at him. The day they'd ridden in the mountains she'd seen for herself how much the horse meant to him. The two of them were true buddies. "No, I haven't heard. Has something been wrong with him?"

"He got a thorn in his foot that day, and it abscessed. But he's doing well now. I'll be able to ride him soon."

"That's good. I know he's special to you."

"Yes. Very special. And thankfully I won't need him until fall roundup starts next month."

"I imagine you and your brothers will be extra busy when that goes on," she commented, while her mind continued to whirl with endless questions.

Why had he been the one to drive her this morning? And why was he behaving as though there wasn't a hard, cold wall between them? Was he trying to make amends so they wouldn't part on a bitter note? Yes, that had to be it. And that was good, she thought. At least she could remember him as the warm and friendly Jack she'd first met at Three Rivers.

"For sure. We'll hire more hands during that time." He looked at her. "Now that I think of it, you didn't meet any of our ranch hands. I wish you had. They're all good men. You'd like them."

The more he talked, the more it felt like a foot was standing in the middle of her chest. "No. I didn't get a chance to meet them. But I figure you and your father are like Blake and Gil. They wouldn't have anyone working for them who wasn't likable and steady."

He agreed, then went on to explain how he and his father had decided to invest a chunk of money into new fencing for the ranch.

"So what will your priorities be after roundup and the fence-building?" she asked.

"You."

At first she thought she'd heard him wrong, and then realizing she hadn't misheard his word, she scooted to the edge of the seat and stared at him.

"Me? What the heck does that mean?" she asked.

Before he had time to answer, she looked out the windshield and noticed that while they'd been talking, the outskirts of Cedar City had slipped behind them and he was still heading south.

"Where are you taking me? Is the airport way out here?"

"No. This is the way to Las Vegas. That's where I'm taking you."

Incredulous, her jaw dropped. "Why?"

For the first time since they'd driven away from the ranch house, he grinned at her. "Other than to gamble and have a fun time, why else do people go to Las Vegas? To get married."

She gasped. "Have you lost your mind?"

"I lost it for a little while. But thank God I got it back. And just in time."

She fell into stunned silence, and he wheeled the truck into a graveled rest area on the right side of the highway.

"Jack, I don't understand," she mumbled painfully. "I..."

He turned toward her. "Oh darling, Vanessa, I'm asking you to forgive me. I'm asking if you're willing to take a gamble on me and be my wife, the mother of my children."

"Marry you?" she whispered the two words in wondrous amazement. "But Jack, how— You said you never wanted to marry!"

He unsnapped his seat belt and leaned across the console in order to pull her into his arms. "That was before I understood what it was like to really love. And I do really love you, Vanessa. It took the reality of you leaving to make me realize just how much I need and want you in my life. How much I want you at my side—for always."

Suddenly tears of joy were sliding down her

cheeks. "Oh, Jack, I do love you! I have from that first night at Three Rivers when we kissed under the stars."

He gently wiped away her tears with his forefinger. "All this time I've been afraid, Vanessa. Afraid to love you, then afraid to let you know that I did love you. You'd been so hurt and disappointed by your ex that I doubted I'd ever meet your expectations in a man. And I didn't think I had a right to ask you to leave your life in Arizona. I'm not sure I'm worthy of that much from you."

She cradled his face with both hands. "Oh, my darling, don't think I'll be sacrificing. If I'm lucky, I can probably find a teaching job within driving distance of Stone Creek. And we can always drive down to Arizona to visit my parents and the other Hollisters."

His lips formed a smile against hers. "The *other* Hollisters. Thank God for my new relatives. If not for them, I would never have found you."

She gave him a long, thorough kiss, then easing her head back asked in a sly voice, "Does this mean we're eloping to Vegas?"

"It does. That is, if you're willing to say yes to my proposal. Or would you rather wait to have a big wedding?"

Shaking her head, she laughed softly. "And risk giving you the chance to back out? No way. When we hit the city, we're going straight to a wedding chapel."

Laughing with her, he smacked kisses over her cheeks and nose and forehead. "Now that we have that settled, the only question left is how many kids we're going to have."

She rubbed her cheek against his. "Well, twins run in your family. Maybe we'll have two on the first try. Or maybe we'll be like Kat and Blake and have two sets."

He grinned. "Hmm. Well, we'll do our best to catch up to them. But whether we have one or five babies, just know that I'll always love you."

"You know, it's a good thing we're going to Vegas," she said slyly.

"Why do you say that?"

With a low, sexy chuckle, she slipped her arms around his neck. "Because I'm one lucky woman."

Epilogue

Halloween night on Stone Creek Ranch turned out to be cold and windy, but inside the den, where most of the family had gathered to enjoy the homemade candy Claire had made for the occasion, the fireplace crackled with a stack of burning logs.

Standing at the windows overlooking the backyard, Vanessa watched in fascination as snow flurries swirled toward the rose garden and sifted over the carefully covered plants.

"You're going to keep watching that snow until you're hypnotized by the stuff and don't know where you are," Jack teased as he walked up behind her and circled his arms around her waist.

"Mmm. I love seeing the snow. And I know exactly where I am. In my husband's arms."

He nuzzled his cheek against the side of her head. "Happy Halloween, darling. You're the best treat a man could ever hope to get."

Happiness bubbled up from deep within her and turned her lips up into a smile. "Isn't it wonderful, Jack? We've been married for two whole months, and our lives are just getting better and better."

"Sometimes I wonder if I should have Cord punch me on the chin just to make sure I'm not dreaming."

Since they'd returned from their wedding in Las Vegas, Jack and Vanessa had been living in the ranch house with the rest of the family. The situation was fine with Vanessa, but Jack wanted the two of them to have a home of their own. Yesterday they'd picked out a spot for the house, and next week a contractor was coming to lay out the foundation.

In the meantime, Vanessa had received word that she'd landed a teaching position at the high school in Beaver. Since the opening had come about because a teacher had abruptly retired for health reasons, Vanessa would be starting the new job at midterm, shortly after the holidays.

"You are happy about me getting the teaching position, aren't you?"

His arms tightened around her. "Thrilled. Your job is as important to you as mine is to me. I'm your biggest cheerleader."

"Well, I've assured Hadley and Maureen that

I'll keep working on the family tree." Turning, she rested her hands on the middle of his chest. "Actually, I'm beginning to think I might have stumbled onto a lead, Jack. I haven't said anything about it to anyone yet. I don't want to raise hopes and then have them fall flat."

"What is this lead?" he asked curiously.

"I've figured out that Joseph Hollister, great-great-great-grandfather to Blake and his siblings, had a first wife who died in childbirth. I think it was assumed that the child didn't survive. But I can't find a record of its birth or death. What if the baby did survive and the maternal grandparents took the child away and raised it elsewhere? That might account for a whole other line of Hollisters."

His brows arched with speculation. "Sounds like you might be onto something. It would be great if you had this figured out by Christmas. You couldn't give Dad and Maureen a better gift."

She gave him a coy smile. "And what am I going to give you, dear husband?"

His eyes twinkling, he murmured, "Gifting me is easy."

He was lowering his mouth toward hers, when Beatrice suddenly called out.

"Hey, you two. You need to come over here and settle a dispute. Mom wants to serve champagne for your wedding reception and Dad says beer."

With a good-natured groan, Jack lifted his head and, with his hand clasped firmly around Vanessa's, urged her away from the windows. "Sounds like we better go do some negotiating."

As they approached Hadley and Claire, who were sitting on a love seat in front of the fireplace, the matriarch of the family was saying, "Beer is fitting for a bunch of cowboys, Hadley, but it doesn't quite measure up for a wedding reception."

Claire had been happily planning a big reception for the newlyweds to be held just before the Thanksgiving holiday, and Jack had remarked that it had been years since he'd seen his mother this animated about anything.

"Most wedding receptions offer more than one alcoholic beverage. Why don't you serve both, Claire?" Vanessa suggested. "That way the men can have their beer, and the women can sip the champagne."

"Your daughter-in-law just solved the problem," Hadley told his wife. "We'll have both. Beer and champagne and maybe a little moonshine if I can find it."

Hadley's last suggestion brought a chuckle from Cordell, who was kicked back in a huge recliner. "Moonshine would liven things up. But I'm more concerned about what we're going to eat."

Standing by the fireplace, Beatrice rolled her eyes and groaned. "You would be, Cord. You eat enough for two people. My concern is the guest list. Are any of the men from Three Rivers coming up for the party? Now, that would be something to look forward to."

Jack gave Vanessa a conspiring wink before he replied to his young sister's remark. "I don't know about the men, but Vanessa's good friend Maggie has already said she's coming up for the reception."

Cordell glanced over at Jack. "Is this friend young and pretty?"

"Oh, Cord, if it's not food with you, it's women," Beatrice said drearily, then glanced hopelessly over to Hadley. "Dad, can't you do something with him? He's a stain on the Hollister name."

Hadley's smile was indulgent as he looked at his young daughter. "If I tried to set Cord on an upright course, then I'd have to set you on one, too. I'm not so sure you'd like that, Bea."

Laughter spattered throughout the group, and then Jack turned his attention to his brother. "Take a word of advice from me, Cord," he said wryly. "You'd better watch your step. This Arizona woman put a wedding band on my finger. What if Maggie sets her eyes on you?"

"Easy," Cord said with a smug grin. "I'll run."

Everyone laughed, and as they did, Vanessa felt Jack's hand tighten knowingly on hers.

* * * * *

Don't miss Stella Bagwell's next book,
The Maverick's Marriage Pact
part of the
Montana Mavericks:
Brothers & Broncos continuity,
coming October 2022 from
Harlequin Special Edition!

COMING NEXT MONTH FROM

H HARLEQUIN
SPECIAL EDITION

#2929 ONE NIGHT WITH THE MAVERICK
Montana Mavericks: Brothers & Broncos • by Melissa Senate

Everyone thinks Shari Lormand and veterinarian Felix Sanchez are a couple. Unfortunately, the guarded widower has made it abundantly clear all he's looking for is a buddy. Shari is afraid she's hurtling toward another heartbreak. But with a little help from the town psychic, she and Felix just might have a shot after all...

#2930 FOREVER, PLUS ONE
Holliday, Oregon • by Wendy Warren

Nikki Choi loves the boisterous family she was adopted into as a baby. But dreams of her own happy-ever-after are dashed when her fiancé suddenly calls off the wedding. Leave it to her BFF Evan Northrup to come to her rescue. But the single dad seems intent on keeping things pretend, while Nikki is shocked to be falling wildly, deeply for her old friend...

#2931 THE DESIGNER'S SECRET
Small Town Secrets • by Nina Crespo

Usually sensible Layla Price stuns herself when she spends the night with a handsome stranger. Blaming it on a freak rainstorm and Bastian Raynes's heroic rescue, Layla believes she'll never see him again. She's only in this small town to end some silly family feud. Except...Bastian's family is on the other end of that feud and Layla's hiding her real identity!

#2932 THE SPIRIT OF SECOND CHANCES
Heart & Soul • by Synithia Williams

Single mom Cierra Greene is determined to succeed in real estate. Too bad her most lucrative property for sale is...haunted? Reluctantly, she seeks out Wesley Livingston, a cohost of a popular paranormal investigation show, for help. Cierra and Wesley try to ignore their unfinished business, but when old feelings resurface, things get complicated...

#2933 A CHARMING CHRISTMAS ARRANGEMENT
Charming, Texas • by Heatherly Bell

Stacy Hartsell thought finding her unborn baby's father was going to be the hard part. Except widowed ex-SEAL Adam Cruz is determined to step up—and his argument that his veteran health care is better than her freelancer plan is a fairly convincing one. Giving in to their feelings *could* put their convenient arrangement in jeopardy...or lead to a second chance to find lasting love this Christmas!

#2934 CINDERELLA'S LAST STAND
Seven Brides for Seven Brothers • by Michelle Lindo-Rice

Despite crushing on his Prince Charming looks, personal assistant Maddie Henry has had enough of Axel Harrington not recognizing her value. Well, this Cinderella is shattering the glass slipper to pursue her dream career! The "Sexiest Man Alive" has two weeks to find a new assistant. And to realize that Maddie is the key to his happily-ever-after.

YOU CAN FIND MORE INFORMATION ON UPCOMING HARLEQUIN TITLES, FREE EXCERPTS AND MORE AT HARLEQUIN.COM.

HSECNM0722

Cierra's lips lifted in a smile that brightened his dark
corner of the coffee shop as she straightened. "Oh, good,
you remember me," she said, as if he could possibly
forget her.

How could he forget Cierra Greene? Head cheerleader,
class president, most popular girl in school and slayer of
teenage boys' hearts.

"Yeah…I remember you." He managed to keep his
voice calm even though his heart thumped as if he'd had
a dozen cappuccinos.

"I was worried because you didn't return any of my
calls." She tilted her head to the side and her thick, dark
hair shifted. Her smile didn't go away, but there was the
barest hint of accusation in her voice.

Wesley shifted in his seat. He hadn't returned her
calls because ever since the day Cierra told him after a

basketball game that she was ditching him for his former best friend, he'd vowed to never speak to her again. He realized vows made in high school didn't have to follow him into adulthood, but the moment he'd heard her voice message saying she'd like to meet up and talk, he'd deleted it and tried to move on with his life.

"I've been busy," he said.

"Good thing I caught you here, then, huh?" She moved to the opposite side of the table and pulled out the other chair and sat.

"How did you know I was here?"

"Mrs. Montgomery," she said, as if he should have known that one of the most respected women in town would give his whereabouts to her. She must have read the confusion on his face because she laughed, that lighthearted laugh that, unfortunately, still made his heart skip a beat. "When I couldn't reach you, my mom called around. Mrs. Montgomery said you typically spend Friday afternoons here. So, here I am!" She held out her arms and spoke as if she were a present.

Her bright smile and enthusiasm stunned him for a second. Wesley cleared his throat and took a sip of his coffee to compose himself. How many years later— fifteen—and he still had the lingering remnants of a crush on her?

Come on, Wes, you gotta do better than that!

He took a long breath and looked back at her. "Here you are."

Get 4 FREE REWARDS!

We'll send you 2 FREE Books plus 2 FREE Mystery Gifts.

FREE
Value Over
$20

Both the **Harlequin® Special Edition** and **Harlequin® Heartwarming™** series feature compelling novels filled with stories of love and strength where the bonds of friendship, family and community unite.

YES! Please send me 2 FREE novels from the Harlequin Special Edition or Harlequin Heartwarming series and my 2 FREE gifts (gifts are worth about $10 retail). After receiving them, if I don't wish to receive any more books, I can return the shipping statement marked "cancel." If I don't cancel, I will receive 6 brand-new Harlequin Special Edition books every month and be billed just $5.24 each in the U.S. or $5.99 each in Canada, a savings of at least 13% off the cover price or 4 brand-new Harlequin Heartwarming Larger-Print books every month and be billed just $5.99 each in the U.S. or $6.49 each in Canada, a savings of at least 20% off the cover price. It's quite a bargain! Shipping and handling is just 50¢ per book in the U.S. and $1.25 per book in Canada.* I understand that accepting the 2 free books and gifts places me under no obligation to buy anything. I can always return a shipment and cancel at any time by calling the number below. The free books and gifts are mine to keep no matter what I decide.

Choose one: ☐ **Harlequin Special Edition** ☐ **Harlequin Heartwarming**
(235/335 HDN GRCQ)   **Larger-Print**
(161/361 HDN GRC3)

Name (please print)

Address   Apt. #

City   State/Province   Zip/Postal Code

Email: Please check this box ☐ if you would like to receive newsletters and promotional emails from Harlequin Enterprises ULC and its affiliates. You can unsubscribe anytime.

Mail to the Harlequin Reader Service:
IN U.S.A.: P.O. Box 1341, Buffalo, NY 14240-8531
IN CANADA: P.O. Box 603, Fort Erie, Ontario L2A 5X3

Want to try 2 free books from another series! Call 1-800-873-8635 or visit www.ReaderService.com.

*Terms and prices subject to change without notice. Prices do not include sales taxes, which will be charged (if applicable) based on your state or country of residence. Canadian residents will be charged applicable taxes. Offer not valid in Quebec. This offer is limited to one order per household. Books received may not be as shown. Not valid for current subscribers to the Harlequin Special Edition or Harlequin Heartwarming series. All orders subject to approval. Credit or debit balances in a customer's account(s) may be offset by any outstanding balance owed by or to the customer. Please allow 4 to 6 weeks for delivery. Offer available while quantities last.

Your Privacy—Your information is being collected by Harlequin Enterprises ULC, operating as Harlequin Reader Service. For a complete summary of the information we collect, how we use this information and to whom it is disclosed, please visit our privacy notice located at corporate.harlequin.com/privacy-notice. From time to time we may also exchange your personal information with reputable third parties. If you wish to opt out of this sharing of your personal information, please visit readerservice.com/consumerschoice or call 1-800-873-8635. **Notice to California Residents**—Under California law, you have specific rights to control and access your data. For more information on these rights and how to exercise them, visit corporate.harlequin.com/california-privacy.

HSEHW22R2

HARLEQUIN
PLUS

Announcing a **BRAND-NEW**
multimedia subscription service
for romance fans like you!

Read, Watch and Play.

Experience the easiest way to get
the romance content you crave.

Start your **FREE 7 DAY TRIAL** at
www.harlequinplus.com/freetrial.

HARLEQUIN

Heartfelt or thrilling, passionate or uplifting—Harlequin is more than just happily-ever-after.

With twelve different series to choose from and new books available every month, you are sure to find stories that will move you, uplift you, inspire and delight you.

SIGN UP FOR THE HARLEQUIN NEWSLETTER

Be the first to hear about great new reads and exciting offers!

Harlequin.com/newsletters

Love Harlequin romance?

DISCOVER.

Be the first to find out about promotions,
news and exclusive content!

f Facebook.com/HarlequinBooks

y Twitter.com/HarlequinBooks

O Instagram.com/HarlequinBooks

P Pinterest.com/HarlequinBooks

You Tube YouTube.com/HarlequinBooks

ReaderService.com

EXPLORE.

Sign up for the Harlequin e-newsletter and
download a free book from any series at
TryHarlequin.com

CONNECT.

Join our Harlequin community to
share your thoughts and connect
with other romance readers!
Facebook.com/groups/HarlequinConnection